P9-DZM-682

Yasmina Reza

ADAM HABERBERG

Yasmina Reza is a playwright and novelist whose plays *Art*, *Life x 3*, *The Unexpected Man*, and *Conversations After a Burial* have all been multi-award-winning critical and popular international successes, translated into thirty-five languages. She lives in Paris.

INTERNATIONAL

ADAM HABERBERG

ADAM HABERBERG

Yasmina Reza

Translated from the French by Geoffrey Strachan

Vintage International
Vintage Books
A Division of Random House, Inc.
New York

FIRST VINTAGE INTERNATIONAL EDITION, FEBRUARY 2008

Translation copyright © 2007 by Geoffrey Strachan

All rights reserved. Published in the United States by Vintage Books, a division of
Random House, Inc., New York, and in Canada by Random House
of Canada Limited, Toronto. Originally published in France by Albin Michel, Paris,
in 2003. Copyright © 2003 by Éditions Albin Michel S.A. and Yasmina Reza.
This translation originally published in hardcover in the United States by
Alfred A. Knopf, a division of Random House, Inc., New York, in 2007.

Vintage is a registered trademark and Vintage International and colophon are
trademarks of Random House, Inc.

This is a work of fiction. Names, characters, places, and incidents either are the product
of the author's imagination or are used fictitiously. Any resemblance to actual persons,
living or dead, events, or locales is entirely coincidental.

The Library of Congress has cataloged the Knopf edition as follows:
Reza, Yasmina.
[Adam Haberberg. English]
Adam Haberberg / by Yasmina Reza ; translated from the French
by Geoffrey Strachan. —1st American ed.
p. cm.
I. Strachan, Geoffrey. II. Title.
PQ2678.E955A6513 2007
843'.914—dc22
2006022057

Vintage ISBN: 978-1-4000-7846-2

Book design by Soonyoung Kwon

www.vintagebooks.com

Printed in the United States of America
10 9 8 7 6 5 4 3 2 1

ADAM HABERBERG

One day the writer Adam Haberberg sits down in front of the ostriches on a bench at the Jardin des Plantes menagerie in Paris and thinks, this is it, I've found the poorhouse position. A spontaneous position, he thinks, you can find it only when you're not trying. One fine day you sit down and there you are, you're hunched in the poorhouse position. He feels at ease in this position; I feel at ease in it, he thinks, because I'm young and there's no onus on me to stay like this. In normal times Adam Haberberg soon bounces back, but these are not normal times for him, a man who's paid six euros to walk a few yards parallel with the Quai Saint-Bernard, then come back again and collapse onto the very first bench, opposite the ostriches in what is undoubtedly the ugliest and least attractive part of the garden.

So, one day, there in front of the ostriches in the Jardin des Plantes, Adam Haberberg sits down. The bench is wet from invisible rain. The two flabby, gray creatures are eating a kind of straw in front of their hut in a totally bare enclosure. The cell phone in his pocket rings. "Hello?" "Did you see the weather?" says the voice. "Enough to make you blow your brains out." "Forget it. That's how it goes." "Where are you?" "In the Jardin des Plantes." "What are you doing in the Jardin des Plantes?" "Where are you?" "In Lognes. Eldorauto car accessories. In the parking lot." "What the hell are you doing in Lognes?" "Waiting for Martine. How's the book?" "Disaster." "Will I see you?" "I'll call you back."

At the brick entrance to the big cats' house the word *shop* looms monstrously. The optometrist, he tells himself, the optometrist was not all that reassuring. On the other hand he was not alarmist. But then would an optometrist be alarmist? Would an optometrist say, Monsieur Haberberg, we can't

exclude the possibility that very soon you'll have lost
the use of your left eye, dear Monsieur Haberberg,
what guarantee have we that when you leave here
you'll still be able to cross the street like before? No.
The optometrist says, the second angiogram confirms
the diagnosis of partial thrombosis in the central vein
of the retina. Showing more hemorraging than in
the first. This is normal. It's normal for the edema
to deteriorate before beginning to be absorbed. It
may take between six months and two years before
becoming stabilized, it could deteriorate, remain
stable or improve. The optometrist also says, you're
lucky, Monsieur Haberberg, you still have good close
vision, you're not seeing things blurred, you're not
seeing them distorted. And he adds, we must also do a
visual field test since the back of the eye you present is
of a type that could give rise to glaucoma; this is only
a suspicion, but the iris is furrowed and we have no
right, you understand, to ignore what might be the
start of something. Adam Haberberg is forty-seven.
A young age, he thinks, at which to see the murkiness
of death winking at him. It had begun with a flickering sensation, it always begins with things like that, he
thinks, a flickering, a buzzing, a smarting sensation,
these barely perceptible things, little alarm bells ringing. He had covered his right eye with his hand and

said to his wife: my vision's blurred. That's all we need, was her comment. The sight in my left eye's all hazy. It's a speck of dust, it'll pass. She didn't give a damn. She'd already left the room, she didn't give a damn about anything to do with him. The word *thrombosis,* modestly articulated a few days later, only irritated her. The word *thrombosis* had swept away any residue of indulgence or understanding within Irène's heart.

Adam Haberberg thinks about Albert out there at Lognes waiting for Martine in the Eldorauto parking lot. He thinks about his wife; he thinks about his eye. He thinks about the catastrophe of his book. He thinks about that animal whose canine teeth project beneath its lower jaw, stooped there in a corner of the garden between two ovals of shrubbery. Solitary, he read on the panel, habitat: the mountain forests of Asia. Solitary, yes, he thought, watching the tailless quadruped trembling as it grazed, but not a solitude like this, the solitude of flat ground, no air, with unappetizing grass and the noise of cars, in that part of the world, shown in red on the panel, which is your habitat, you can see the sky through gaps in the darkness, I've never written about mountains, he thinks. When it comes to the footpaths and trails I love, I'm tongue-tied.

Adam Haberberg was no longer fond of his book. He even viewed it with loathing. Had pride led to this? A more or less honest attempt, he conceded, to explain the disaster? What had to be admitted was that the book, of which he had once (and until recently) been tentatively fond, fond indeed in spite of or because of this tentativeness, was suddenly no longer dear to him, rejected, even regarded, in fact, as just one more pile of shit amid the proliferation of useless piles of shit and that this feeling was sincere, with the subtle proviso that it was hard to identify the moment when it had crept up on him, at what stage of the disaster it had taken over, and whether what was occurring was the onset of lucidity or a salvage operation. Was it the event (or nonevent) as a whole, or one particular verdict? A judgment that could be regarded as relevant or as emanating from a voice held to be relevant? Irène, who had not contested the word *disaster,* had accused him of giving credence to the social disaster, so that the social disaster had mentally transformed itself into a literary disaster, this slippage in Adam's mind from social to literary disaster disgusted Irène, who saw in it nothing but betrayal, cowardice, and abject spinelessness. Théodore Onfray writes that your book is a pile of shit, Irène had complained, so now I, your wife, who told you it was good, lack true vision.

I'm worth nothing and my opinion's worth nothing. Equally extreme, it transpired, was Goncharki, who found it positively unnatural for anyone even to glance at a column written by someone like Onfray. Your bitterness is nauseating, Goncharki had said, and your doubts even more so, you worry about being rejected by the very people you abominate, you've clearly got your back to the wall. I can only regret, he had said, that you didn't see fit to assume a furious air in my presence, which would have secured a certain degree of loftiness for the two of you, you and your book.

Since neither Goncharki nor Théodore Onfray suffer from thrombosis or glaucoma—and as far as he's concerned Adam doesn't believe in this glaucoma anyway, what kind of fate would assail the same man and the same organ twice over?—neither of the two is qualified, thinks Adam, to pronounce a relevant judgment on the way of the world. Why let one's peace of mind be eroded by these petty barfly pundits, which is, of course, unfair to Goncharki, who's a genuine skeptic. As for the glaucoma, Adam simply doesn't believe in it. Let us grant the thrombosis, he thinks, I hadn't foreseen the thrombosis, but let us grant the thrombosis. But no way am I going to have both a thrombosis and glaucoma. Accustomed as I am, he thinks with nostalgia, to minor ailments not one of which was taken seriously.

Children in parkas run along beside the railings. A wind gets up, ruffling the feathers of the sparrows and pigeons in the enclosure. This thrombosis is a leap into old age. After the first visit to the optometrist Adam had looked up the word *thrombosis* in the dictionary: the formation in a living being of a clot in a blood vessel or a cavity of the heart. Why should it have specified in a living being? If not to emphasise the abnormality and the danger? Irène had shrugged her shoulders. She was exasperated. Irène no longer loved him. He reproached her with no longer loving him. To which she would reply that this was an unjustified reproach, since to cease loving is not to be culpable. He would pounce on this statement, exclaiming, you see, you admit it, you don't love me anymore. To which she replied, I'm speaking generally; you can't blame someone for ceasing to love. He would persist: so you admit it, in your horribly cold manner, you've just admitted you no longer love me. She would accuse him of conversational perversity, she would say, it suits you to revile me. He would reply, I'm not reviling you, I'm stating a fact. That was how most of their exchanges went. Irène was an engineer at France-Télécom; she used to leave around eight in the morning and come home, exhausted, around nine o'clock in the evening or later. He blamed her for working a galley slave's hours, which transformed him into a nanny (they had two boys of five and eight), he blamed her for lacking any serious angst, the same as all her friends in the public services, if only, he would say, you understood the difference between physical fatigue, he would say, and mental fatigue—and it was, he knew, a terrible injustice that Irène never sought to correct—you come home, he would say, and you can draw a veil, whereas we, meaning we artists, are obsessed day and night, there's no rest for us.

Adam calls Albert again. "That's it, then, the diagnosis of thrombosis is confirmed." "Shit." "Partial thrombosis in the central vein of the retina." "Shit." "Cardiovascular ultrasound scans, clotting tests, tests for diabetes, cholesterol, et cetera. All I have is a genetic anomaly." "Hold on, I'm letting Martine in." "Hyperhomocysteinemia." "What's that?" "A thing that causes thromboses. They're going to do a visual field test too. I may have glaucoma." "I didn't hear that." "I may have glaucoma." "Glaucoma? Why would you have glaucoma?" "The optometrist says maybe I have glaucoma." "As well?" "As well as the thrombosis." "You're not going to have both of them?" "Why not?" "Right. When will I see you?" "Tell Martine it's crazy to work at Lognes." "I'll tell her." "Especially at Eldorauto." "I agree." "Tell her I'd like to meet the genius who invented that name." "OK." "Has she read my book?" "She's going to read it." "Tell her I've got a thrombosis." "An Animalis truck is blocking my exit from the parking lot."

She'll never read my book, that wretched Martine, thank God, what does she know about literature, thinks Adam. But at least let her buy it, that'll make a sale. She won't buy it, of course, Albert will lend her his copy. Frustration at every turn. The only difference between success and failure, Goncharki had said, is movement. If something's on the move it creates a buzz. You get a little relief from the gloom of life.

For years Goncharki had been writing a kind of essay with a metaphysical thrust inspired by the life of the gangster Meyer Lansky. Adam, who was also fascinated by Lansky, had heard Goncharki utter the name over dinner. People who could sustain a conversation on the subject were rare and Goncharki had accorded him a friendly welcome to that night's entourage. Their discussion had taken off on the principle that it was better to be Meyer Lansky than so-and-so or so-

and-so. They had begun with their fellow writers and then moved on to politicians, to so-called philosophers, to footballers, to corporate bosses, to the pope, and each time it was better to be Meyer Lansky. The final conclusion was that it was better to be Meyer Lansky than the rest of humanity combined. From this accord a relationship was born, reinforced by a shared passion for the game of chess (until a stupid argument comes to deprive them of this pastime). Goncharki smoked two packs of Gitanes a day and could fall asleep at night only completely drunk. By a curious phenomenon of self-discipline, although no pressing reality obliged him to remain on course, he would begin drinking only at about seven in the evening and by the time he was hauling himself under the covers, he had knocked back some five pints of alcohol, including a bottle of whisky. In the past Goncharki had published a couple of crime novels in the well-known Série Noire and a pamphlet called *Cultural Zones,* subtitled *A Survival Manual.* His wife had fled with their daughter when the child was six. She was a dentist in Tours and every month transferred a payment of nine hundred euros into his account. He wrote books for two popular fiction series, Blade and Vice Squad, and latterly, having for some unknown reason taken a violent dislike to

Richard Blade, only Vice Squad titles, he sometimes translated political texts from German for the European Documentation Center. He scraped a living. Why didn't the thrombosis attack him? Why is it my eye the blood's clotting in, thinks Adam, I'm a man in perfect health (one's day-to-day complaints have nothing to do with one's health). Why is it me embarking on this appalling process of drugs and hospitals? Why not Goncharki, who's totally abused his body for decades, who has bloodshot eyes and nothing more to lose? I'm only forty-seven, he thinks, as he watches the absurdity of the strutting ostriches through the railings—what's the point of wings if they can't even manage a tiny flutter—I'm young, I'm too young for the world to be blotted out. The optometrist had given him Veinamitol, a vein tonic in the form of a powder taken orally, recommended for the treatment of hemorrhoids. You can always go on taking it if you like, Professor Guen had said, when consulted after the first angiogram, a remark that smacked of resignation and gloom. Prior to the Veinamitol they had prescribed aspirin—the Veinamitol had seemed more serious; despite its hemorrhoidal mission, it had sounded like something capable of soothing the red corpuscles and strengthening the blood vessels. Up until that unfortunate remark of the professor's Adam Haberberg had knocked back the Veinamitol with conviction. Now he took his two packets halfheartedly with a certain resentment, even. The truth was he went on taking the Veinamitol lest, if things got worse, he be blamed for leaving off the Veinamitol. He continued with the Veinamitol superstitiously. Professor Guen had added to the treatment two Spécialfoldine pills a day. But the Spécialfoldine had nothing to do with the Veinamitol, or even the retinal thrombosis itself. It was meant to assist in correcting the genetic irregularity known as hyperhomocysteinemia. The Spécialfoldine, Guen declared, should compensate for the folic acid deficiency, which could lead to further thromboses elsewhere. It was a treatment for the general constitution. It could not be counted on to boost the morale. Adam is about to call Albert again. He forgot to mention that weekend in Normandy, on the Cotentin Peninsula. The Cotentin was his idea. He'd had the idea of spending a weekend on the Cotentin because you need to have ideas like that from time to time. You decide happiness is possible, a couple of days is nothing, it's within easy reach, you tell yourself it's really the minimum a family needs, to go off for two days and collect seashells at Saint-Vaast-la-Hougue. At the first service station Adam had bought the younger boy a water pistol, a purchase Irène had disapproved of. She'd confiscated the pistol and retreated into a hostile silence. Fifty miles down the road happiness had vanished. At the service station the other families looked happy, the other families in the cars they passed looked happy. Was that pistol so serious? The pistol was serious—such was the sense of Irène's silence—it demonstrated his general thoughtlessness. A couple, Goncharki had once said on an inspired day, is like a house. It gets put together over a period of time, the foundations, the walls, the ceilings, you reinforce the roof, the doors, and the windows and then it's finished, you can't shift anything anymore. You can give it a fresh lick of paint, you can make a few home improvements here and there but as for the whole bulk of it, you can't shift it anymore. Adam doesn't call Albert again. Albert's with Martine. Without Martine, Adam would have said: I forgot, catastrophic weekend on the Cotentin. And hung up. Without Martine the remark held water. Without Martine, Albert would have called back: I never liked the Cotentin, you need to cut it out. And hung up. Without Martine they would have had this vital exchange. Albert has Martine, who massages his feet and cooks him veal sweetbreads, I have Irène, who hates me. Do you want a wife who massages your feet and cooks you veal sweetbreads? he thinks, contemplating the aggressive redbrick walls of the big cats' house. Adam admits the water pistol was a mistake. The water pistol was an open invitation to madness in the car. But madness in the car was better than the silence of death, in any case madness had quickly taken over in the back, even without the water pistol, and soon in the front as well, for no one can endure shouting and absurd arguments combined with an absurd refusal to react and he in his turn had started yelling absurdly when the older boy had whined, look what he's just done, Daddy, he's made crumbs all over the car, let's play at spitting, the younger one had said, he's gross, the older one had shouted, hitting him, he's spitting at me. I'm doing a hundred in the rain, Adam had bellowed, if you don't stop that racket I'll smash us all to smithereens. Madness had reigned in the car after the water pistol had been put away in Irène's handbag, while she continued to stare silently and with an uncommonly stiff neck at vistas of warehouses, billboards, and corrugated iron. Why had she not simply said, boys, the pistol will travel in my bag, it will reappear on the beach at Saint-Vaast-la-Hougue, in a mild and even slightly complicit voice, a voice that would mildly have implied, he's a terrible one, your daddy. But the mild voice no longer exists.

In the kingdom of the couple the mild voice with no
memory is no more. Adam thinks again about that
analogy between couples and houses, an idiotic analogy, like all analogies, what can Goncharki know
about couples, drunks have no business putting forward theories on any subject, even though drunks
have a greater lust for theories than anyone else.
Apparently the ostrich is a great seducer, he's just read
this. The male ostrich has a harem, which he apparently assembles after performing an irresistible court-
ship display. And you, poor creatures, thinks Adam,
observing the pair alone behind the wire netting, do
you occasionally make some kind of wild display, you
poor creatures, trembling there under the drizzle in
that cement enclosure? Irène would have liked to live
in the shadow of a man. For Irène a successful life
would have been subordinating her own to a man's
success. That was what Irène had dreamed of, to be a
powerful man's bondwoman. Being a vilified writer's
wife was for Irène the worst possible scenario. Before
he was vilified, Irène had supported him with all her
strength, she had stimulated and encouraged him, she
had everywhere extolled his excellence, and she had,
Adam thinks, truly believed in his excellence. Could
she go back on this? Could she accept society's verdict
without going back on her own? Not least because

society's verdict doesn't come all at once. Society's verdict is insidious. The first book had had a mainly favorable reception. The second had been totally demolished. The latest had been ignored by everyone except Théodore Onfray, who had alluded with a note of skepticism to the miraculous praise accorded to the first. Irène was trapped, it was her duty to maintain solidarity with the vilified poet against the world. She whose most secret dream was to sacrifice herself for a man. To sacrifice herself for a man who won recognition would have been a kind of achievement for Irène, she would never, in any case, have spoken of sacrificing herself, since she would have sacrificed only the social part of herself, her useless part. Instead of which she'd had to resign herself to the path in life for which her randomly oriented studies had prepared her. After the Higher National Telecommunications School and several years of professional experience, while pregnant with their first child, she'd done an MBA on space radiocommunications systems and was now working as project head at France-Télécom's Research and Development Department in Issy-les-Moulineaux. As for a brilliant career, Adam thinks there on his bench, an expression that often comes to mind, and in exactly these words, Irène Haberberg is the one who's had one.

"So how was Saint-Vaast-la-Hougue?" says Albert, who's just called him back. "Catastrophic." "Of course." "Where's Martine?" "In the supermarket." "Are you outside?" "Yes." "So you've got fuck all to do." "What do you mean I've got fuck all to do? What about you? At least you ate some oysters?" "Sure. They're the best on the whole North Atlantic coast." "Who told you that?" "My friend in Cherbourg." "The best are Cancale." "Saint-Vaast-la-Hougue." "Cancale or Marennes-Oléron." "Oléron is way down south!" "The best are Cancale or Oléron, everyone knows that." "OK, you're getting on my nerves. *Ciao*."

A woman emerges from the shop. At the top of the steps to the big cats' house a woman has emerged from the shop. She sets down her two bags and opens a folding umbrella. Adam watches her walking down the steps and as she walks down the steps it looks as if she's watching him. Adam turns back toward the ostriches. It looks as if she's coming toward me, he thinks, staring hard at the ostriches. He takes a sidelong squint. She's coming toward him. A woman on the verge of smiling, encumbered with two bags and an umbrella, is approaching him. Marie-Thérèse Lyoc. Marie-Thérèse Lyoc, Adam thinks. And immediately thinks, no, not Marie-Thérèse Lyoc here, today, no. And then he thinks, for such is fate, yes it is.

"You recognize me?"

She stands there, unable to get over it and bursting with energy.

"Marie-Thérèse Lyoc."

You couldn't call her ugly, thinks Adam. You couldn't have called her ugly thirty years ago, nor today either, he thinks, what you could have called her at the time, as now, was insignificant, even though at the time, he thinks, it would not have occurred to anyone to describe her at all, if it occurs to him today it's because by appearing from nowhere, by taking the form of a happening during the course of a day set aside for lethargy and gloomy thoughts, Marie-Thérèse has suddenly become somebody.

"This is great," she laughs.

"Yes."

There's a silence. And then a sudden squall blows everything toward the Crimean pine, including the umbrella, which is transformed into a feather duster. Adam gets up to help her, trying to put the ribs the right way round. Marie-Thérèse laughs in the wind, struggling with the fabric; he doesn't hear her very well as she says, You see, I've not changed, clumsiness incarnate!

"You don't need it, it's stopped raining," says Adam. The umbrella resumes its shape and the wind blows itself out.

"I know. In fact I never use an umbrella. I generally have a little rain hat. And the day I forget my rain hat, there's a howling gale, my hair's blowing all over my face, and I run into Adam Haberberg."

You run into Adam Haberberg, himself bald, puffy, soon to be blind in one eye, my God, he thinks, how time wrecks us.

"So, Marie-Thérèse," he says with a start, "what's new, Marie-Thérèse, a thousand years on?"

"You want some hot news? I need glasses. That's a fact, from this morning."

"What kind of glasses?"

"For farsightedness. That's the truth. Do you wear glasses?"

"No."

"What frightens me is that this is only the start." She's wiped the damp bench with a tissue and sat down beside Adam. "I can still read everything, you know, I get slight headaches, there are times when I have to frown but I can read everything, and I have the feeling that as soon as I start wearing glasses it's going to get worse in no time at all. The optometrist says no, but everywhere you look there are people who start wearing glasses and within a year they can't even decipher a restaurant menu."

"Well, that's true. . . ."

"But you're going to tell me, OK, we all come to it."

"Well, yes."

"And you, what about you?"

"Well . . ."

"Are you married? You have children?"

"Two."

"And what do you do?"

"I write."

"Books?"

"Yes . . ."

"Great."

"Yes . . ."

"Are you making it?"

"I'm making it," he says, thinking, What vulgarity.

"Great."

"And are you making it? What are you doing these days?" thinking, did I ever know what she was capable of doing, did I ever know she existed.

"I sell merchandise."

On top of the thrombosis, the failure of the book, and the weekend on the Cotentin did he need Marie-Thérèse Lyoc? On top of the rain, the wind, and the wretched animal from the forests of Asia, after considerable efforts to keep his head above water, did he need Marie-Thérèse Lyoc selling merchandise? Marie-Thérèse opens the larger of her two bags.

"I work with zoos, amusement parks, and museums. We're in a zoo here, so it's all customized to relate to animals; I have mini fridge magnets, traditional fridge magnets, magnetic words, a pocket flashlight, look, an unbreakable ruler, there's a giraffe motif on this one but at Giverny there'd be a picture by Monet, a ballpoint, same thing, a different theme for each site, all kinds of pencils with heads, here you've got a parrot, a bear, they used to do little animals but they don't do them anymore, they get all this stuff from Asia."

Adam switches on the pocket flashlight, he bends the unbreakable ruler, he stares at the eraser, the little notebook, the key ring, and he seems interested in the box of mini magnets, she tells him I'll give it to you, she says how many children do you have, he says two, she says right I'll give you two of them and two bookmarks, the cat and the frog, she says you're a writer, would you like a ballpoint, here, Gustav Klimt, that should suit you, Adam tries the ballpoint in the air, he finds it unpleasant at the end of his fingers but he says terrific, that shop didn't exist, Marie-Thérèse says proudly, then one day I came to the menagerie, I met the person in charge of promotion but the menagerie had no structure for buying products. I pestered them for months and that's how the shop came into being, Adam says fantastic. She closes up her bag of samples, which is like a box of toys, in a few minutes, he thinks, the world has changed, the spectacles, the eraser, the parrot, he puts the mini magnets, the bookmarks, the ballpoint, the soothing world of Marie-Thérèse Lyoc into his pockets, he feels like a sick person who sees people on the sidewalk in the distance and envies the ordinary passerby. "And what were you doing here?"

"Nothing. I was watching the ostriches."

"Oh my! I've been coming here for months and I never noticed the ostriches."

"I see."

Marie-Thérèse smiles into the void. She doesn't seem perturbed by this disjointed exchange. He turns toward her, finding really nothing to say to her, then smiles as well and she becomes radiant, and Adam Haberberg feels a mounting inner confusion. He says, I've become bald, haven't I? She says, just a touch. A great big touch. Just a touch but it suits you. I ought to get up and walk away, he thinks. I ought to get up and say good-bye and good luck, Marie-Thérèse. He says, I've put lotions on it, I've battled with it, but you can see how it is. She bursts out laughing, Oh my, what a fuss you make about it! He has a memory of her, he sees her again in a corridor at the Lycée Paul-Langevin, in a time now gone forever, in a corridor he'll never walk in again, wearing her pinafore dress, day after day wearing that same pleated dress he remembers, Marie-Thérèse Lyoc, the faceless girl, trailing along in the same class as him for several years, and with whom he would finally walk down the street or board a bus. One day she turns up with you in a café because Alice Canella, whose slave she has become, says, make a space for Marie-Thérèse, so you make a space for Marie-Thérèse, who doesn't exist, who's neither brunette, nor blond nor anything. She says what kind of books do you write?

"Newsstand literature."

"What's that?"

"Popular fiction series."

That's what he'll do in future, he thinks, thinking about himself as if he were a character escaping from his own control. And it's so easy to say it, he thinks, I manufacture pulp fiction, as you might say, I manufacture chair covers, it's direct, it's frank. It's anonymous. Marie-Thérèse says, so what are popular fiction series?

"Series, you know the kind of thing? Bob Morane? The Famous Five? Remember?"

"Oh yes, the Famous Five."

"Francis Coplan, Agent OSS 117."

"Vaguely."

"They're series."

"I see."

"Well, there you are."

On the deserted pathway a child walks past with its mother. One of the ostriches straightens up and fluffs out all its feathers. Look, cries the child, it's pooped! Oh yes, says the mother. The ground in the enclosure is covered in pools of water, the birds make their way around them, everything is gray. In one of the first Blade stories Goncharki wrote, Adam remembers, Goncharki had used the words *tommy gun*. Don't ever say tommy gun, the publisher was incensed, you say machine gun or machine pistol, you're writing for men who'll be reading it in the train on the way back to barracks. The men who read me, Goncharki had said, are the guy on the station platform, the guy alone in his room in the provinces, all loners.

"And Alice Canella?" says Adam. He would never have wanted to say, and Alice Canella. In fact it was the last thing he would have wanted to say. Luckily the cell phone rings.

"Riec-sur-Belon." "What the hell's that about?" "Ouistreham." "Saint-Vaast-la-Hougue." "No one's heard of them." "How do you know?" "Martine asked the fishmonger." "Tell her the fishmonger's crap." "You still in the Jardin des Plantes?" "Yes . . . with a woman friend of mine." "Do you make all your assignations at the Jardin des Plantes?" "I didn't have an assignation. Where's Martine?" "At the dry cleaner. Have you just picked her up?" "No." "Pretty?" "No." "Screwable?" "By you, yes." "Introduce me." "You've got Martine." "What's that to do with it?" "OK. I'll call you later."

Don't repeat the question, he thinks, don't say, and have you seen Alice Canella again?

"And have you seen Alice Canella again?"

"Didn't you hear?"

"Hear what?"

"Alice is dead."

Above the entrance to the building there's a kind of Soviet-style bas-relief. From where he stands Adam can see a woman carrying a stag suspended by its legs from a pole. Alice Canella is dead.

"When?"

"Twenty years ago."

He also believes he can detect the sound of a fountain away somewhere on the right. What I should do, he thinks, is go and see if there really is a fountain behind those bushes.

"She threw herself out the window."

Marie-Thérèse Lyoc discreetly presses her legs together. She leans on her bag of samples and endures the wet wind without stirring. Marie-Thérèse doesn't dare say any more. But then she says, she was heavily into drugs, you know, after that she kicked the habit and became fat.

"Fat?"

"Yes. Really fat."

Up in that attic room, thinks Adam, Alice Canella used to dance with her long blond hair and her slender legs, we listened over and over to "Little Wing," she danced to "You Got Me Floatin' " in front of the boys smoking on the bed, we were the kings of the future.

"I can't imagine her fat."

"Oh yes."

"Marie-Thérèse."

"Yes?"

He puts his hand to his left eye. He has the feeling that a moment ago things behind the eye suddenly deteriorated. It feels to him like a maelstrom, a generalized extravasation—he recalls the word—caused, he thinks, by the rupture of the collateral vessels, that he ought, he reproaches himself, to have had analyzed and subjected to laser treatment, having been perfectly well alerted to the fact that this temporary circulatory network would be of poor quality and shouldn't be relied on to sustain the white heat of life, nor its deep shadows, nor life itself. All right? says Marie-Thérèse. He takes his hand away and stares at one of the two ostriches. It has an endearing head, he thinks, a long, slender neck and a tiny head in relation to its body, he can see it clearly, he notices, just as clearly as before, he takes the ballpoint out of his pocket and can see that clearly, likewise the frog bookmark, he sees them clearly, just as clearly as before, apart from the unreality engulfing the whole day. The disturbance hasn't had any physical conse-quences so far, he thinks. He can get used to internal spasms, if he has to, provided they don't interfere with the functioning of his senses, provided every-thing remains in good order.

"Yes, all right," he says.

"What are you doing now?"

"Now?"

"Right away. We're not going to stay here."

What do you mean, we're not going to stay here? Could he have foreseen a more extravagant remark?

"I'm going home now, you're welcome to come if you're free."

"Where do you live?"

"In Viry-Châtillon."

"Where's that?"

"Beyond Orly airport, heading south."

Adam thinks again of Albert waiting in the parking lot at Eldorauto in Lognes. Why does he remain dangerously silent? There are thousands of ways of avoiding Viry-Châtillon. He must be at death's door if he's hearing himself being offered a visit to Viry-Châtillon.

"Do you live alone?"

"Yes."

On the other hand, he thinks, what's the alternative to Viry-Châtillon? The children in front of a cartoon, sprawled across a floor strewn with the remnants of Kiddy-Treats and Napolitain cookies, the rude shock of switching channels, the shouts of fury mingled with the start of the news bulletin, Irène's shouts when she gets back because they're not in bed, because they're not wearing slippers and dressing gowns, Irène's exhaustion, the battle over their teeth, the battle of bedtime, the lesson in motherhood from Irène leading her heroic, solitary life at his side, her only conversation being about domestic matters. Alice Canella is dead. Alice Canella became fat and threw herself out the window. So is it yes? says Marie-Thérèse.

"Why not?"

"Great."

She gets up.

"I have my Jeep here."

"You have a Jeep?"

"It's that little Wrangler."

She points to a black Jeep on the parking lot. Marie-Thérèse has a Jeep.

"Are you allowed to park on this lot?"

"Oh yes," she says, "I have a permit. I even drive the car into Versailles. I've had my photo taken there in the summer, because when a woman in sunglasses with a car like mine drives through the gate of honor, the Japanese say, Hey, that must be someone important."

There is indeed a fountain behind the bushes. A hidden fountain with an ancient, patinated lion towering above it. I should call home, Adam thinks. He moves away from the sound of running water to call the babysitter. He's cold. The daylight is beginning to fade. In the Jeep Marie-Thérèse says, it guzzles quite a lot of gas, eighteen miles to the gallon, but that's normal for a big engine, the interior's completely washable, you can run a hose over the inside, it seems strange the first time, I've always liked four-by-fours, I don't act like a four-by-four in my car, but I feel safe in it, I do so much driving in the course of a year.

Adam feels at ease in the Jeep. He's happy to be high up, happy to be driven. Irène never takes the wheel when they're together. He's happy to be alone in the world, heading toward Viry-Châtillon. In the car driving over to the Cotentin he'd had the thought, this family, just an ax and a moonless night, I'll soon polish them off. Irène had remained mute until Caen. The older boy wanted to hear "Les Loups" for the fifteenth time. Is that Madonna, Daddy? the little one said. He's a complete moron, this boy, that's Serge Reggiani, you can tell it's a man singing. Now listen to this, children, Sonata Number 5 in F Minor, the most beautiful sound in the world. I generally take the throughway, says Marie-Thérèse, but we'll take Route Nationale 20 because I have a little shopping to do in Sceaux. At this time of day it doesn't take much longer. I want "Les Loups" right now! Learn to be silent, children, and look at that castle, it'll be gone in a flash. I can't wait till we get to the thingy where you're going to buy a pocket ball. Here's what happens in *Halloween,* right, there's this girl, right, she's brushing her hair and her brother comes in and he's got a knife hidden. I don't give a damn, I don't give a damn about your stupid pocket ball and *Halloween,* I'm listening to Bach, who reassures me of the fact that a superior humanity exists. Thanks to

you I'll have swallowed sixteen vanilla-flavored lico-
rice cough drops and you're supposed to eat only
one every two days! They turn into the Boulevard
de l'Hôpital. Passing the Pitié-Salpêtrière Hospital,
Adam thinks about his very first publisher, the only
man who ever had faith in him. It's no small thing in
life, a man who has faith in you. It gives you strength
and courage. Adam recalls him, his tousled hair, his
implants sticking up in all directions, his hospital
gown split up the back over his white shorts—in a
garment like that you can talk only standing up face-
to-face or in profile, otherwise you're in trouble.
There he was in his room in the cardiology unit at the
Pitié-Salpêtrière, somewhere in the depths of those
buildings, saying, everything's fine, guys, the medics
say I'm going back to Paris at the end of the week.
You never *went back* to Paris and here I am heading
toward God knows where. Look what's become of
me, was that what you had in mind? A man who has
faith in you, that's something that keeps your head
above water. Adam thinks about his publisher, now
dead and gone. Dying had smartened him up. The
funeral director's staff had dressed him in a new jacket
chosen by his wife. He looked heavy. Heavy on his
bed, absurdly smartly dressed with gleaming shoes.
Does one have to be dressed? thinks Adam. Who'll

dress me? With a bit of luck it could still be you, Irène. Because we won't do anything, people don't split up, people don't split up, they stay together locked in tedium and dementia. Marie-Thérèse has stopped at a traffic light. The windshield wipers slide groaning across the glass, night falls, it's hard to tell if it's still raining or not. How does she arrive at that hairstyle? thinks Adam, noticing the presence of a woman at the wheel of a red car beside him. Does she sit down and say give me a Joan of Arc haircut? So are you well-known? As a writer? Excuse me for asking, says Marie-Thérèse, I'm always behind the times. These days, Marie-Thérèse, as you should know, but you do know it, as your question sadly proves, the worst calamity is to be nobody. As a result of this, Adam continues, not knowing from where exactly inside him these orotundities are issuing forth here in the Place d'Italie, everyone produces books, this still being the least hazardous recipe for moving from nothingness into the light. Nowadays fame via litera- ture is the most widely shared aspiration, a new social reflex, you see. Some succeed, some fail, I personally have failed. I'm a failure. Marie-Thérèse turns right. They proceed down the Avenue d'Italie. Adam stares at the signs as if he were passing through a foreign city. The word *Naturalia* strikes him. Marie-Thérèse drives the Jeep in silence—it's clear she likes driving her Jeep—then she says, what have you failed? She turns a distressed face toward him. In the distance Adam becomes aware of the Charléty Stadium in a misty glow. Marie-Thérèse pushes buttons. Adam accepts the fog. There we were, walking along that street in the Suresnes district and Alice Canella stopped and said to me, you're my best friend, Adam. I'd have given her, if she'd wanted it, my time, my dreams, my life. She wanted nothing, you're my best friend, Adam, she said. What have you failed? asks Marie-Thérèse. And he hears himself replying, maybe nothing that was worth the trouble.

"What a strange way to talk. We're still young," says Marie-Thérèse.

"I don't think so."

"We're not even fifty."

It's imperative, thinks Adam, to leap out and escape into the traffic. Instead of which he extracts a little notebook from his pocket and records Marie-Thérèse's remark with the Gustav Klimt ballpoint. Then he says, where do the zoo animals go at night? Do they take them in?

"Why should they? They stay outside in their natural state."

"They're not in their natural state."

He again pictures that solitary animal from the forests of Asia in its pathetic enclosure, feeling an affinity for this dejected creature. With a bit of luck the mist will have blanketed your pathetic enclosure, the noise of cars along the Quai Saint-Bernard will be like a distant rumble. In the mountains one can rise above the mist, he thinks, in the mountains one climbs high into the clouds and at every step the landscape changes, as do the light and the smells and the weariness and the joy that have no place in time, for they are things outside of time, he thinks, now stationary on the Boulevard Kellermann. I've never written about the mountains. When it comes to the footpaths and trails I love, I'm tongue-tied. So what's this thing about popular fiction series? says Marie-Thérèse.

"I don't write popular fiction series. It's a friend of mine."

"I see."

"He's called Jeffrey Lord. He generally writes about ten books a year."

"That's a lot."

"Yes. That's why I sometimes give him a hand. I write one or two for him."

"I see."

Adam studies Marie-Thérèse's remark in his notebook again. *We're not even fifty.* He has circled the

We're. He circles it again. Adam was putting his latest book behind him. In seeking to break all ties with his personal emotions, he told himself—not wanting to succumb to the abject fashion for autobiography— he'd broken all ties with himself. He'd calculated too much, planned too much, given too much thought to literature. A real writer gives no thought to literature. A real writer doesn't give a damn about literature. He'd wanted to make his mark, which is another way of flaunting one's ego in the marketplace. He'd lacked humility, he knew. The result was an account of a mother-son relationship written in the third person from the mother's point of view. Two fatal mistakes as far as he was concerned. And what a mistake, he thinks, to assume Théodore Onfray is motivated by malice. Maybe your only friend, the only one who took the trouble to read you and form his own opinions, the only one to deplore your artificiality and feebleness. Adam had not entirely lied to Marie-Thérèse Lyoc. Goncharki had developed an aversion to Richard Blade, the intergalactic traveler who provided his livelihood. Pressed and harassed, as he put it, by the publisher and unable to deliver a title on schedule, he'd jokingly invited Adam to stand in for him. After two and a half weeks, a record time for a beginner, during which he'd done nothing but remain hunched over his computer, eating dried fruit and energy bars, Adam presented Goncharki with *The Black Prince of Mea-Hor*. Goncharki had skimmed through the manuscript and declared it to be far and away the best of all the Blade books he'd ever written. And not only the best he'd ever written but quite probably, although he'd read only one of them at the beginning and had no memory of it, the best of all the Blades ever written in America or anywhere else. You're the real Jeffrey Lord! he'd toasted him. Who's Jeffrey Lord? Adam had asked, not knowing what nom de plume he'd just assumed. They'd wept with laughter and Goncharki had risen to his feet, thundering at the whole bistro in Churchillian tones, because he was going through a Churchillian period, *We are at war! Now, we are condemned to work each other to ruin, and will TEAR your African empire to SHREDS and desert!* Under Adam's pen the intergalactic hero had, of course, moved out of line a little from his usual persona and this subcontracting had at once been spotted by the *editorial team*. Had it not been for Goncharki's charm and the objectively excellent quality of *The Black Prince of Mea-Hor,* the affair might have ended in tragedy. Up to seven o'clock in the evening Goncharki was good at managing things. On the very same day he'd negotiated his own exit from the Blade series, his recruitment into the Enforcer series, which he'd had his eye on, and his replacement by Adam Haberberg, who seemed unbelievably at ease in the galactic universe. Four titles per year, three thousand euros gross per title, such was the basis of the offer made to Adam without further ado. An offer he'd not been able to respond to and one which would have shattered him had not the news of the thrombosis arrived to sweep away the existential shock of it. Thrombosis. What a horrible word, thinks Adam, raising his hand to his eye and remembering that the pain, although reduced, is still there. I've just finished a biography of Leonardo da Vinci, says Marie-Thérèse.

"Oh yes."

"I really like biographies."

"Quite right."

"When I've a meeting, I really have to target. It's important for the customer to say to himself, she doesn't just sell anything to anybody. Take the meeting I had at the Clos Lucée, the house François I gave him. I really focused on the target beforehand so as to maximize my chances of opening up an account with this customer. I'm lucky to have a professional occupation that opens me up to fresh horizons. Right, I'm going to pass, that one's getting on my nerves. Some specialists say this is the best off-road vehicle in the world, you know. The sales representative of today, if he wants to succeed, needs to look beyond the confines of his own little business."

"Of course," says Adam, noting Marie-Thérèse's jeans. And her sneakers. They go with the Jeep, he tells himself. The hairstyle, too, more up-to-date than the face. The rest, the coat, the scarf, the handbag, are reminiscent of that see-through figure in Suresnes long ago.

"The salesman, as people picture him," she says, driving past the BaByliss building, "the guy at the end of his tether, eating alone in the restaurant with his suitcase, there are still lots of those, but I'm not like that at all. I've positively bloomed in my profession. The buyers know that."

The men who read me, Goncharki used to say, are the guy on the station platform, the guy alone in his room in the provinces, all loners.

"The people who succeed in this profession," Marie-Thérèse continues—God knows why she's charging into the breach like this, thinks Adam, but maybe she sensed his look—"are people who are open to the world and pleasant-looking. What's enabled me to succeed in my profession is being genuine, being authentic. Those girls in their suit-skirt-and-heels at trade fairs, you don't see much of them as the years go by, only the authentic people stay the course. You need to feel good about yourself when you go somewhere. I walk into a museum, it's a museum where they're not working with me, I need to make them feel the need. If I want to persuade them to create a *sales outlet* for my merchandise I need to go in with a presentation that's about more than the outlet. They need to get the feeling I'm not there to set up an outlet at all, even if they know very well that setting up an outlet there is the bottom line. The buyer wants more from this relationship than his little sales outlet, the purely commercial presentation is a thing of the past."

Low apartment blocks, gray buildings, pink apartment blocks, in brick, in tiles, and Darty and Cora and Mondiale Moquette, a nondescript road through the fog, which has left only a few trails of mist behind, little suburban villas in the dusk, and Speedy and Laho Supplies and billboards all the time and the sign for Montrouge and the sign for Bagneux through the rain on the window. And Marie-Thérèse Lyoc bursting with energy inside the warm Jeep. Marie-Thérèse heading homeward, who knows it all by heart and doesn't give a damn, who's not the type to think that life's decor should be fairyland. Marie-

Thérèse repeating words he doesn't understand that run into one another and dance like the gleaming raindrops.

"Do you remember Serge Gautheron?" she says.

"No."

"Dark hair, not very tall. His father had a sports equipment store at Rueil, Serge Gautheron, can't you picture him?"

"More or less."

"We got married."

"You're married?"

"I'm divorced now but we were married for eight years."

I can't cope, thinks Adam, I can't cope with this grotesque piece of information, I'll focus on the road, a road entirely dedicated to the car, a road of garages, gas stations, inspection and repair garages, I'll focus on new and used car sales showrooms, I'll focus on body shops, places where they sell tires and spare parts, I don't want to hear about Serge Gautheron's and Marie-Thérèse Lyoc's lives, I don't want to know anything about these ghosts from the past. He recalls wandering around in a scrapyard at Carrières-sur-Seine looking for a white fender for a Passat. He recalls the waste ground, the guy in his cabin that smelled of tobacco and the dog that surged up from nowhere, barking, at the end of a very long, endless chain.

"I even have a picture of the two of you," says Marie-Thérèse, "a school photo taken in the eleventh grade, I think."

Of course she's kept all the class photos, he tells himself. The same set of class photos his mother always kept, the way she kept his teeth, blackened with age, in a metal box. Those class photos in which he invariably appears sad and ugly, sadder and uglier he used to think, with every passing year. While each time the others looked better in those photos, there was always something dubious about me, he told himself, the phony smile, the badly parted hair, something phony about my posture. Not one of those class photos was any good, he thinks, and my mother kept them all, every year approving of my freakish appearance, uncritically approving of her boy's progress from grade to grade, keeping everything, teeth, exercise books, Mother's Day gifts, only to end up, now I'm an adult, with a total lack of interest. Adam doesn't want to see the class photo with Serge Gautheron in it. When you say Serge Gautheron, he knows, you're saying Alice Canella, you're saying Tristan Mateo. Alice Canella is dead. I don't want to see myself standing alongside Tristan Mateo and Alice Canella again.

I don't want to contemplate such an epitaph on my youth in the company of Marie-Thérèse Lyoc. I want the Bourg-la-Reine road sign, I want Peugeot, Champion, and Volvic, I want to take my car in for an inspection, I want to buy wall-to-wall carpet and wallpaper. Alice used to go on vacation with Marie-Thérèse, Adam recalls. When they came back Marie-Thérèse gave herself airs because she knew things no one else knew. That she might have had a love life of her own never crossed anyone's mind.

"So were you together already at the lycée," he says, suddenly finding the idea piquant.

"Ha, ha," Marie-Thérèse laughs. A completely asexual laugh, he thinks, an incongruous little throaty laugh, there she goes again, he says to himself, giving herself airs again. I need to make a detour to the Château de Sceaux, just to drop off a package, she continues, turning right down a tree-lined avenue.

Marie-Thérèse walks through the darkness toward the château. Adam has stayed in the Jeep in the paved parking lot. The cell phone rings. "It's me," says Irène. "Maria tells me you're not going home." "No." "What are you doing?" "I'm with an old school friend." "Marvelous." "It's true, I swear." "Where are you?" "At Sceaux." "At Sceaux?" "And then I'm going to Viry-Châtillon." "You can do what you like,

I don't give a damn. Did you talk to the children?"
"No." "Well at least call them." "OK."
Adam calls his sons. The rain has stopped. The park
looks beautiful and the château too. I must come here
one day with the children, he thinks, as he talks to
the little one, wondering how many times in his life
he's had the thought that one day he must do this or
that with the children, knowing he never would.
"And how do they live?" he asks the older boy. "By
hunting . . ." "Yes. By hunting and . . . ? Something in
the water?" "Fishing." "Fishing and . . ." "I don't
know, Daddy, I'm fed up with it. I can't do homework on the phone!" "And gathering. And what's
the difference between history and prehistory?" "Oh
gee, Daddy. Writing." "Writing. Well done. Prehistory charts the progress of mankind *before* writing
appears." "My serial's just starting." "The earliest
forms of writing are very old, you get the first rudiments of writing in three thousand BC. It's very
important for you to understand evolution and know
your way around. I don't want you to do what I
did, which was to go directly from Neanderthal man
to the Mesopotamians, I jumped straight from the
hairy guys in caves to the Assyrian princes in their
gilded chariots, what's that noise, why's he yelling?"
"He fell over with the floor lamp." "What's Maria

doing? Why did she let him play with it?" "Stop yelling, you jerk, I can't hear a thing." "Is he hurt?" "Of course not, Daddy, you know he cries about nothing. My serial's starting." "Sweet dreams. Do a bit more on the harpoon and the assegai." "Bye, Daddy, I love you."

Here in the paved parking lot at the Château de Sceaux, in other words utterly remote from every-where, in other words to hell and gone, in other words where no obligation or logic has brought us, we feel almost at peace, he thinks, and as if enjoying a respite from life. By taking art into the marketplace, Goncharki had often reiterated, that most con-temptible of crimes, people have convinced every Tom, Dick, and Harry that he can be an artist. Tom, Dick, and Harry have no cause to be suspicious, they live in a world that says to them every day, express yourself, give full rein to your ego. Tom, Dick, and Harry, Goncharki had said, suffer the same torments as the authentic artist, vulnerability, anxiety, the dif-ficulty of creation, since all this derives from the man and not from the artist. They're quickly admitted to the community of their peers, unaware that there can be no such thing as a community of artists, for the artist and above all the writer, Goncharki had said, although you and I both know we're talking about a minor branch of the genre, is a loner who has no desire to mingle and recognizes neither peers nor colleagues. In our society Tom, Dick, and Harry are given no guidelines. You can't blame them for believing they're the real thing. When you write pulp fiction you have no horizon beyond death. You're a mercenary, you no longer have a name, you go on endlessly repeating a gesture that leaves no trace. Adam draws a circle in the mist on the window and looks out to where there's nothing to see. Bye, Daddy, I love you. How much longer these sunlit words? On the street, when he's going off to school in the early morning, the older boy calls out I love you to his father who's watching him from the window as he crosses. At the corner round which he'll vanish he calls out I love you over the heads of the passersby, over the cars, and his father up there leaning out blows him a kiss and repeats the words in a low, embarrassed voice. A father who could have been one of a different kind, a father who, he too, in a sort of way, is a Tom-Dick-or-Harry father, knowing very well that this I love you is not addressed to him, Adam Haberberg, the man standing at the window, unshaven and feeling old, but to his figure throughout the ages, due throughout the ages sometimes to be *the best daddy in the world* and sometimes the most wicked. One day, he thinks, this child who knows nothing about you and prefers TV serials, will no longer be heard calling out I love you in the street. One day the boy staggering along the sidewalk with his bulky schoolbag and the man giving him a friendly wave, wrapped in his cloak of uncertainty, will be erased by time.

Adam dials Albert's number.

"I'm in Sceaux." "In Sceaux?" "After that I'm going to Viry-Châtillon." "Very nice." "So what are you doing?" "I'm on the stairs. I'm taking out Martine's King Charles spaniel." "She has a King Charles spaniel?" "These dogs are the ugliest things in the world. This guy's a four-legged thyroid deficiency." "You're going out walking on your own with the King Charles spaniel?" "Seventy-five percent of the time I carry it in my arms, it doesn't like walking. I put it down when it wants to shit." "Why does she have a King Charles spaniel?" "She likes King Charles spaniels." "You can't stick with a woman who works in Lognes at Eldorauto and has a King Charles spaniel." "You're right." "Dump her. I've got someone for you." "Who?" "Marie-Thérèse Lyoc." "Big boobs?" "Not bad." "Introduce me." Adam puts

the cell phone back in his pocket. By the tentative
evening light shadowy figures are emerging from
the park. Adam puts his hand over his eye. He thinks,
I'll need to explain this evening's happening to the
optometrist. I'll need to find the exact word, I'll need
to direct him with precise care toward a fresh appre-
ciation of the situation, I'll need to find the exact
word and then, for want of being able to select one
that comes just below it in the scale of impact, for the
calibration of words is crude, I'll need to tone it down
with an adjective, for it's essential, Adam considers, essential not to put the optometrist in a panic.
Doctor, what I suddenly experienced was a disturbance . . . no . . . a spasm of pain . . . no, not a pain . . .
a dislocation, yes, a *type* of dislocation, as if, Doctor,
my blood vessels were parting company with the
artery and dispersing aimlessly into aberrant places.
Now could this be that famous extravasation process
you told me about, the very name of which haunts
me? My vision hasn't been affected by it, that's a good
sign, isn't it, Doctor, as if my eye wanted to know
nothing about what was being plotted behind its
back, as if my eye were following a kind of metaphysical false trail that arose above the organs, declaring,
you'll go on seeing to the very end, even if you're no
longer irrigated, even if nothing binds you to the

roots of life you'll see, until your last blink, the world will be clear. Note, Doctor, that I should like the same thing to happen to the whole of me. For I experience this feeling of dislocation in the depths of my being, as if its component elements were no longer connected either to one another or to a unique self, as if at any moment and anywhere at all, a fragment of myself could go floating off toward the outer margins where I'm lost. Doctor, do you believe the world can remain clear if you're traveling toward the future with no prospect of joy, because you're no longer whole enough to grasp it? The other day we set off, my children, my wife, and I, to spend a weekend at Saint-Vaast-la-Hougue. As I was heaving the suitcase and bags out of the elevator various tales of exile and headlong flight came into my mind and it occurred to me, Doctor, that these must have been less painful than this departure for the Cotentin, I reflected that ineluctable fate is easier to bear than the duty to be happy. As I pick up the vacation suitcase at the foot of the stairs I'm picking up the burden of life. My first publisher was a gentle man, not very tall. He was bald and had hair implants that were an utter failure. Yesterday I passed the hospital where he died. I hope you don't have a problem with this little digression, Doctor. After all, who is to say that the thrombosis that concerns us today has no connection with my beginnings as a writer? My first publisher had faith in my future. That's no small thing in life, someone who has faith in your future. It gives you spirit and courage. His diary, written in the Pitié-Salpêtrière Hospital, which his wife photocopied, contained these words, "At the end I bear helpless witness to the frenzy of self-destruction that is overwhelming my heart. . . . It is the body, our body, that is the ultimate and principal foundation of our being. . . . Adam Haberberg brought me a radio, one of those actions of great thoughtfulness that makes the night bearable." So, maybe he swallowed up my future with him? My future crumbled to dust in the pit, along with one of those handfuls of earth cast onto the wood. You prescribed Veinamitol for me, Doctor, when I told Professor Guen of this he made a little gesture with his hand, one of those gestures that signify blithe indifference, and said, you can always go on taking it if you like. I'm naive enough, Doctor, to think a patient needs to have faith in the virtues of his medicine for it to be effective. I'd read the label on the Veinamitol, I'm a great reader of labels, and I'd felt encouraged by the clarity of what it indicated. Professor Guen blew Veinamitol sky-high for me. I go on drinking it superstitiously and also because I couldn't confront the prospect of this malfunction without some kind of support, however absurd. And let me remark in passing that his Spécialfoldine, a medicine for pregnant women, is not going to motivate me. To abandon the Veinamitol, Doctor, would be to admit *officially* that nothing can be done, either for this eye or for the other one, which might well be attacked in its turn, or for any other part of my body where a blood vessel might choose to become obstructed. On the label it said, "increases the *resistance* of blood vessels, reduces their permeability." I liked *increases* and *reduces,* two honest, dynamic verbs and, above all, I liked *resistance.* This label gave me authority for a semblance of optimism, Doctor, it acted like the resolutions we make at the start of the new year when we tell ourselves this year you'll do this and you'll no longer do that, when we declare what lies within our own willpower, faced with the chaos of life. Indeed, Doctor, do we not owe to Veinamitol the fact of having overcome the phenomenon of dislocation? That's right! That's what I told myself yesterday during the crisis, I even stopped off at a pharmacy, as I was a long way from home and didn't have my evening dose with me. What does this Guen know about general medicine? What do these highfliers know when it comes to prevention? You're on familiar territory, Doctor,

when you say Veinamitol you know what you're talking about, and I find it unacceptable that this Guen,
whom you were so keen to send me to, already *fortified*
by your prescription, should denigrate it with such
frivolity. I have the feeling you like me, Doctor. Or
maybe I should attribute your solicitude to the fact
that when a man has a vascular problem at my age, the
prognosis is not good. But even so I sense in you,
when I come, a certain pleasure in seeing me. I'm pre-
sumptuous enough to believe it's not every five minutes you see a patient with whom you can joke and
even laugh at the worst, with whom you can talk literature and music, and I appreciate this desire for culture in you, something that normally exasperates me
about people in the circles I move in. For you to like
me, Doctor, is as essential to my recovery as the
Veinamitol, for the man who arrives on your landing
and rings your bell is a man trembling with fear. He'll
make jokes, he'll discuss books and music, he'll hold
forth about fishing if need be, or football, or do-it-
yourself, anything, Doctor, which might enthrall you
and render untimely some announcement of the
darkness that awaits me. To remain what he is, that is
to say invulnerable, the Prince of Mea-Hor mustn't
be liked by anyone. I wrote *The Black Prince of Mea-
Hor* in two and a half weeks, an anonymous book that

can be found only at train stations and some news-
stands. By portraying myself, how shall I put it, *a con-
trario,* through this character, who needs to remain
free of the affection of others, Doctor, I've put more
of myself into this work, written to order, than
into any of my other books. I've constructed the
anti–Adam Haberberg, an anti–Adam Haberberg cre-
ated by my own pen, who gives me the courage today
to reveal my weakness to you, to say to you, like me,
Doctor, protect me, Doctor, save me.

Marie-Thérèse is running. I haven't been too long,
she says, you're not cold? She presses the controls and
drives off. You don't look very well.

"I'm fine, Marie-Thérèse."

"You know, it's really great we met up."

"Yes."

"So, to answer your question," says Marie-Thérèse,
playfully, as they drive down the road from the
Château to rejoin the Route Nationale, "no, we were
not together at the lycée."

"Who?"

"Serge and me."

"I see," says Adam, striving vainly to conjure up a picture of Serge Gautheron.

"We weren't even particularly friendly. He was on
the rugby team with Tristan, I don't know if you

recall, we used to go to cheer on the team at Bagatelle Park. Then I happened to meet him again when I was a trainee with Canon, three years after passing my diploma. That was the odd thing."

"Very odd."

"When we got married we took over his parents' store at Rueil-Malmaison."

"It didn't go well?"

"Us or the store?" she laughed.

"Both. The store."

"The store went fantastically well. But we opened another one in the Bercy 2 shopping mall that never took off. We had to starve Rueil to keep Bercy alive. At a shopping mall, the customers behave quite differently. If your salesclerk is good you make a healthy profit, if she's no good you make nothing. We had the two stores for two years, it was a disaster. We sold Bercy and Rueil folded very soon after that."

"How did you end up in Viry-Châtillon?"

"I made some contacts at Bercy and I was offered the job of managing one of the Caroll ready-to-wear outlets at Juvisy-sur-Orge. I lived in Juvisy first and then Viry."

Adam attempts to study Marie-Thérèse's breasts. Nothing can be seen beneath her overcoat. The Rue d'Antony has everything one could wish for, a hairdresser, a locksmith, an optician, a greengrocer, a pharmacy. I need to buy something at the pharmacy, he says.

It was difficult all on my own, says Marie-Thérèse, turning in front of the Buffalo Grill, I wasn't used to managing a boutique on my own, managing the staff, selecting the stock, being quick to replace it to satisfy customer demand, you've got to take care of everything, if you're not around you're just playing at it. I wanted to be more independent, to have more freedom in my schedules. After three years I resigned and for almost two years I had no work. Through the window, sheds, more sheds, cranes, more cranes, detached houses, Maxauto, Auto Distribution, Hertz. Through the window, warehouses, pylons, heathland streaked with electricity. They're driving along the throughway toward Savigny-sur-Orge. The new box of Veinamitol is on Adam's knees. Marie-Thérèse is talking about her life. The edema *may* take between twelve and eighteen months to be absorbed, the optometrist said. What Adam understands is that the edema may take between twelve and eighteen months to be absorbed comma and may equally never be absorbed. The word *may* filters this rhythm into Adam's awareness. It's a remark that leaves the way open to tragedy. Why didn't the optometrist say the edema *will* take et cetera, because he refuses to employ an affirmative form of words, and why does he refuse to employ an affirmative form of words? Because the absorption of the edema is in itself uncertain, because nothing's less certain than the absorption of the edema. When the optometrist says the edema may take between twelve and eighteen months to be absorbed, he's saying we must wait several months to know if the edema, this stubborn and unpredictable entity, will oblige us by being absorbed at all. We, that is to say you, me, Professor Guen, and the whole medical profession, will have to wait patiently for the time it takes our planet to make a complete revolution around the sun in order to know how the stars are going to incline, in which case, thinks Adam, why not cut to the chase and consult an astrologer. Seven thousand francs net plus incentive bonuses when I started, continues Marie-Thérèse, now if all goes well I earn about four thousand euros. In winter there are not so many tourists at the sites. When we move into the September to March season, which is the worst, I bank on the Japanese. The Japanese travel all year round. All the business we do in France is my doing. Thanks to what I've done in France the company, which is American, has taken on a commercial manager in Spain and another in Italy, they've built up a

whole business in Europe from nothing. At the start I
was hired to sell publicity items. They hired me on
the first of January five years ago. By March I hadn't
done a single deal. The Americans are people who
want results and no messing around. As it happened, I
opened my first account on a visit to Versailles with
my godson and that gave me the idea of specializing
in historical sites and switching to souvenirs instead of
publicity items. Then I opened another customer at
Chantilly and after that the whole thing took off like
a rocket. All the business in France is my doing. That's
great, says Adam. It is, isn't it, it's great. I just love my
profession. It's the first time in my life I've positively
bloomed like this in a job. Fog is still passing them and
a little rain as well. Adam delights in being ferried
along amid darkness, rain, warmth, the dreary out-
skirts. Marie-Thérèse takes off her coat. An Albertian
bosom, thinks Adam, and is within an ace of calling
him when he realizes he cannot speak. A heavy and
prominent bosom, of which he'd no recollection,
never, in any case, having had an appetite for heavy
and prominent bosoms, unlike Albert. Adam thinks
back to that last great drama with Irène. Perhaps the
final drama, he tells himself. *I'll send you my courier,*
Adam had said to Albert on the telephone, referring
to Irène. On her way to Issy-les-Moulineaux Irène

used to pass the Rue de la Convention, where Albert lived. A courier with small boobs, Albert had joked at the other end of the line. He says a courier with small boobs, Adam had stupidly repeated. Screw him, Irène had replied. He says he'll take a look at them all the same. That'll be the day, Irène had remarked frostily. *But you'll need your glasses,* Adam had quipped into the handset. Screw you, Irène had said, other people have no complaints! And she left the room slamming the door. What do you mean, other people have no complaints, what exactly does that mean, other people have no complaints?! Adam had yelled, pursuing her to the other end of the apartment. Do you have any idea, Irène had wept, lying prone on the bed and turning the face of a demented woman toward him, do you have any idea of the vulgarity of this conversation? Don't change the subject. I want to know who these other people are, I want to know the meaning of that remark immediately. Do you find it normal to discuss your wife's breasts on the telephone?! Irène, you've given yourself away. You can't begin to imagine what I'm capable of now! Do you find it normal to joke about my breasts with a stupid prick who likes only whores and manicurists, a notoriously brainless scrounger who eats sprats for breakfast?! I don't give a flying fuck about Albert, don't change the subject!

Say you're sorry, Irène had bawled, down on your knees and say you're sorry, say I'll never discuss my wife's breasts with anyone ever again! I should kill you now, Adam had replied. So what are you waiting for? Irène don't push me! Given the life we lead you might as well go ahead! she'd challenged him, kneeling on the bed and offering her neck. Adam hears her voice saying go ahead, squeeze, squeeze, he sees her legs twitching, he hears the little boy's voice saying, what's happening and his own commanding, get out, get out, shut the door. And then the older boy appears and says you're nuts and starts crying, followed by the little one and Adam wants to murder the lot of them.

If you don't understand self-destructiveness in a man, you don't understand men, he remembers saying, during the hellish discussions that follow crises. Better stark tragedy, he thinks, than these nauseating postmortems. You had to understand this mania for talking, this mania women had for always wanting to talk. This ignoble need for explanations. Considering how rare and insipid their sexual encounters were it would make sense if Irène had a lover. Adam resisted this bitter hypothesis. Adam wanted no talk of this bitter hypothesis. And if an access of madness or violent behavior overcame him, he didn't want to talk

about it. Madness yes, discussion no. Irène charged
him with irrational jealousy. Where will this irrational jealousy lead you? she said. Adam didn't take
irrational to mean groundless, he took it to mean
absurd, given that the ties now binding us are mini-
mal. A spurious jealousy, he thinks, there in the
Wrangler Jeep, that's what he takes it to mean. A terrible word, he thinks, there in the Wrangler Jeep, that
he could apply to his entire condition, for a man must
be recognized for what he aspires to be, and who am
I, he thinks, staring out through the windows at the
darkness sullied with fog, if not a spurious paterfamilias, a spurious writer, in other words, he thinks in the
Jeep idling in the traffic on the A6 throughway, a spurious man? Do you have children? he says to Marie-
Thérèse.

"No, sadly, no."

"Would you have liked to?"

"Yes."

"Why didn't you?"

"That's how it was."

"Didn't Serge Gautheron want them?"

"That's not it."

"So you weren't able?" he says, knowing he should
have stopped two questions earlier.

"That's not it."

"So what happened?" he asks, made impatient by her hushed tones.

"I lost the baby, twice."

"You had two miscarriages?" he insists, irritated by her tone and the word *baby*.

"Yes."

"For what reason?"

"They don't know. Often there's no reason."

"You didn't try again?"

"Yes."

"I didn't hear that."

"Yes, I did."

"And you didn't try with other men?"

"Yes . . ."

What's the point of all this mawkishness, these hushed tones, what's the point of all this miserliness with words? Life is cruel, OK, no point in laying it on thick with a tremulous voice, thinks Adam.

"That didn't work either?"

"No . . ."

First find your man who wants to give Marie-Thérèse Lyoc a child, Adam says to himself. But no, he thinks at once, at the school gates you can see dozens of Serge Gautherons and Marie-Thérèse Lyocs, the truth is that Lyocs and Gautherons proliferate, you can even, he tells himself, regard Lyocs and Gautherons as prototypical parents, nonentities who marry one another, leaving the school benches behind only to congregate outside the gates, the sidewalks seethe with Lyocs and Gautherons, these modern folk, energetic, jocular, ultra-concerned. Marie-Thérèse is my age, thinks Adam. At forty-seven, Marie-Thérèse Lyoc can say good-bye to that child. Good-bye to that child, thinks Adam, just as I'm saying good-bye to fame, sooner or later, he thinks, we say good-bye to the future, we embark on the time when life no longer makes any demands on us, when we'll no longer be called upon to be fathers, mothers, lovers, writers, beautiful, positively blooming, happy. We sit down on a bench and find ourselves in the poorhouse position. One fine day you sit down and that's it, you couldn't give a damn about being Adam Haberberg or Marie-Thérèse Lyoc, you know very well that it's all the same in the end, like being Alice Canella, what good did it do her to be Alice Canella only to end up obese and broken on the ground. Marie-Thérèse has switched the windshield wipers on to full speed. And what's the purpose, my God, he asks himself, of this expedition in this absurd Jeep, behind zigzags of water and light, toward this Viry-Châtillon, whose very name oppresses me. I see a lot of my godson, says Marie-Thérèse, maybe she's said other things in the meantime that Adam missed, but at least she's resumed a normal tone of voice, he notes. He lives in Soisy-sur-Seine, it's farther away, more to the south, with his mother, who's my best friend, she's an instructor at the control tower at Orly. He's eleven, my little godson, he's called Andréas. Guess what he wants to be later on?

"Pilot?"

"Not at all."

"Terrorist?"

"Dentist."

"So is he a bit odd, this child?"

"He's mad about teeth. He's been mad about teeth for years. Now he has bands on his teeth he wants to be an orthodontist. For his birthday we had to find him an articulated skull. But he wanted a real one with uneven teeth. The trouble with the plastic skull is that it has perfect teeth. He wants to do experiments, he wants to take impressions, he wants to make a dental plate. I've done some research, you can get skulls from the cemetery at Montrouge, the grave diggers there sell them on the quiet, you just have to pass yourself off as a student. I don't know if I ought to buy him a real skull. It's a problem. What do you think? Is it healthy for him to have a skeleton in his room at the age of eleven? Especially as he reads books only about vampires and the living dead."

"It's healthier than wanting to be a dentist."

"I don't think it's good for him to be able to regard the human body as a toy. And I think he should be taught respect for death. It's important for children to have a notion of what's sacred. Speaking personally, I wouldn't want someone to violate my skull so it could end up on a shelf beside a Game Boy, along with a set of dentures. On the other hand, I understand his curiosity, he's a child drawn to the sciences, he wants to handle the material, he wants to study the real thing. He's not satisfied with the plastic skull. Now just look at that, it's terrible, isn't it, as soon as it rains we get into traffic jams. The plastic skull is ideal man, the model. It isn't man. What interests you at the moment, I say to Andréas, is the mechanism, the way things are put together. Man is something you'll have all your life to explore, Andréas. Man's imperfections, you'll have your whole life to correct them. You want to study a jaw that's been used, you want teeth that have chewed—he wants teeth that have chewed— you want mandibles that have moved up and down, but I tell him you forget that behind all that there's someone who's traveled through life. Inside that box, my dear, I tell him, there were dreams and ago- nies and we don't know where those dreams and agonies have passed on to, what's become of the fer- ment that was within. When we went to Versailles and Chambord, which you loved—he loves castles, especially Chambord, he loved Chambord on account of the staircases—I tell him, you went into the bedrooms and corridors and great halls and all these rooms were empty, and it could have been boring for a little boy, that succession of empty spaces, without any human trace, but you said to yourself that's where the king slept, that's where he looked out the window and saw that forest, how many times did he walk up these steps, and likewise the courtiers and the soldiers, and you respect these spaces, Andréas, because they've seen what you'll never see, because they housed worlds you'll never know. A real skull, I tell him, is the same, it's not a tool, my dear, it's an abandoned room, it's an enigma."

Why me, thinks Adam, why does she tell me all this? The wretched child has plunged into dentistry prior to embarking on full-scale perversion, it's perfectly plain that sooner or later that boy will end up first dismembering his victims and then freezing them, a boy who wants to be an orthodontist at the age of eleven, who wants a skeleton for his birthday and on top of all this, he tells himself, has to endure this flood of moralizing (which is enough to drive anyone insane).

"Marie-Paule," he hears, picking up the thread of the

argument God knows where (who is Marie-Paule?), "considers the whole thing is between him and me, she has no qualms about a real skull, for her death is death, she couldn't care less about it, she wants to be cremated, if people dig up bones, even to sell them, it doesn't shock her, it's a trade like any other, she says. What is it they're selling, a carcass that would have disintegrated over time, there's no longer any human element in it. You do as you like, she tells me, you're the one Andréas asked for a skull, you gave him a plastic skull that's already cost you a lot, if you have scruples there's no need for you to go any further, Marie-Paule, I tell her, I want to do what's best for him. All the same I find it a bit odd for a mother not to have any scruples about such a delicate matter. No?"

"Yes."

"So what is what's best for a child, do we know what's best for a child?"

"No."

"No! But, even so, you do have a slight idea I hope!" she says in consternation.

"Yes, of course," Adam laughs stupidly, for he no longer knows what it is he's just said no to. I should have jumped out of the car on the Boulevard Keller-mann, he thinks, even at Sceaux or Antony, taken advantage of buying the Veinamitol and escaped before being trapped on the throughway. A succession of mistakes, thoughtless moments of inertia, he thinks, all contributing to predestination. It was written that I should go to Viry-Châtillon, Alexander to Persia, me to Viry. There's not a single person in the world, he tells himself, who knows I'm in this car at this spot. And there's not a single person it would interest, who might say, where's Adam, what's he doing right now, is he happy, sad, alone? Irène has lost interest in me, the children are busy, my friends . . . have I any? There's no one in the world, he thinks, who might feel a pang at my absence. Irène wants to be cremated, too. So does Goncharki. When the undertakers were laying out his father in the coffin, he'd remained glued to the door. He'd heard a series of alarming and gruesome noises and had found his father in the casket reduced by a good quarter. Being claustrophobic, Goncharki wanted none of that for himself. Compression, imprisonment, vermin to boot. Such was the prospect, so: cremation. Meyer Lansky had ended his days in a tiny apartment with no view. A man who'd prided himself on being more powerful than U.S. Steel. What good had being Meyer Lansky done him? Only to end up wandering through the torrid streets, lonely and sick. Whether he was buried in Miami or in Jerusalem, in accordance with his unfulfilled wishes, what difference would it make? So whether he's cremated or his skull ends up amid the toys in a child's bedroom, does that change the color of his life? For years Goncharki had been writing *Meyer Lansky's Tomb*. A secret celebration, a secret ode to men who don't know how to be loved. Do you still have your parents? Marie-Thérèse asks suddenly.

"Yes. I still have my parents."

"Are they well?"

Does she know my parents? thinks Adam.

"Yes, they're well," he lies.

"Do you see them?"

"Not very often. They live in the provinces."

"Whereabouts?"

"In Libourne."

"Where's that?"

"Near Bordeaux," thinking, what's it to her? And also thinking I ought to question her in return, but I don't give a good goddamn about her parents, just as I don't give a damn about her whole life.

"And you, how about your parents?" he says.

"My father's still alive. He still lives in Suresnes."

"And your mother?"

"My mother died when I was ten."

"Excuse me."

"Do your children see them?" Marie-Thérèse resumes.

"Who?"

"Your parents."

"Not a great deal."

"That's a pity."

"No."

"Why?"

"Because my parents aren't interested."

"It's mean to say that."

"No."

"It's a shame for children not to know their grandparents."

"They do know one another."

"Not to really know them."

"Excuse me, Marie-Thérèse, but what do you know about it? Why all these clichés? What if the grandparents are utter jerks?"

Marie-Thérèse considers. Then she says, you're exaggerating.

"Will we be there soon?"

"Very soon. We'd have got there by now if it hadn't been for those traffic jams. What'd you like to eat? I've got a little piece of beef in the freezer. I could do a little roast of beef with carrots. Or a gratin dish. Or, this is simple but it's my specialty, I could make you a good potato omelette."

"An omelette, yes."

He says, an omelette, yes, and a little farther on the sign reading VIRY-CHÂTILLON-FLEURY-MÉROGIS hangs there. I'm going to eat an omelette in Viry-Châtillon with Marie-Thérèse Lyoc, he thinks. He looks at his hands resting on the box of Veinamitol, hands aged more than the rest of his body, a little swollen, a little inert, but inoffensive hands, hands no one misses, he says to himself. He thinks about his children sprawled in front of the television and feels a faintness coming on, as if he were immensely far away, as if he'd lost times beyond retrieval. He thinks about the boys in their pajamas, beached on the carpet, among over-turned toys, fragments of cake, candy wrappings, yogurt cartons, two animals tangled together, watch-ing videos, commercials, and all kinds of hideous, yelling images, pell-mell, totally alone in their own way, he tells himself. And he tells himself the older boy hasn't learned his homework, he tells himself the older boy doesn't take school seriously, and the little one ought to be in bed, he tells himself Maria would do better to tuck him in and tell him a story instead of leaving him to rot in front of the television, which she's watching herself, chewing gum, her ear glued to her cell phone, he tells himself the older boy doesn't use the electric toothbrush he ordered, that the book *The Conquest of the New World* remains unopened, that the older boy couldn't give a damn about the conquest of the New World, and all these things of the most trivial importance that wreck his life as a man night after night, he thinks, these absurd concerns that in normal times he regards as evidence of his failure, now here, in the Wrangler Jeep, as it plunges down the ramp leading off the throughway, seem to him to constitute the heartrending substance of life itself. I must go back to Paris, he thinks, just as the Belgian brasserie, Léon de Bruxelles, appears out of the middle of nowhere, I must go back at once, Marie-Thérèse, please do a U-turn, go back onto the throughway, I must go back home, I must put my boys to bed, I must wait for my wife Irène, I must make the best of my children and my wife, I'm forty-seven, in a few years' time all that will have gone up in smoke, I haven't time to eat an omelette in Viry-Châtillon, the best is over for me, as it is for you, and the best, you see, soon comes down to nothing, take me home quickly, I'll put on my pajamas, I'll roll into a ball with the children in the double bed, we'll wait for Irène, laughing under the covers, all three of us in the dark, and we'll give her a surprise when she gets home.

The Jeep runs down a little slope. At the bottom, on a billboard, can be read YOUR APARTMENT IN VIRY.

Adam closes his eyes. At once a glittering ankle boot appears, motionless in the dark. Adam opens his eyes, reads, WITH PICTURESQUE VIEWS OF THE LAKE, and closes them again. The ankle boot is there, right in the middle, and it's green. Adam opens and closes his eyes several times. The ankle boot's still there, more or less fluorescent. Adam closes first one eye, then the other. No ankle boot. The ankle boot appears only when both eyes are closed. An ankle boot, he notes, that ultimately vanishes, but reappears at the next lowering of the lids. Maybe I'm becoming hysterical, thinks Adam. The way things are going, he thinks, shouldn't I approach Guen directly? Is it best to approach the top man directly, or continue on a semipsychoanalytical track with the doctor who's treating me? And why should I have to grapple with this dilemma over the treatment, in addition to the illness itself? A mysterious assault has now been added to the phenomenon of dislocation, Doctor, the effects of which have not, by the way, completely disappeared, each time I close my eyes a green and highly luminous ankle boot appears. I say ankle boot, Doctor, but I could as well say sock, in truth it's a kind of medieval shoe, with a long point at the end of it, weren't they known as *piked shoes,* Doctor? So every time I close my eyes I see a green fluorescent piked shoe in the middle of the darkness. Is this the famous gap in the retina you and Professor Guen hinted at? Could this be the appalling *macula hole* you and Guen alluded to? You see, Doctor, if the ankle boot had appeared without any preliminary I might not be in this state of panic, but it appeared in the wake of the phenomenon of dislocation, which, you'll remember, had not in itself caused any change to my vision. What alarms me, Doctor, is that there's a logical sequence to this. If my retina's torn, and my feeling is that it is torn, we must admit that the dislocation was the prelude to the tear. We fear the worst and the worst happens. I don't know if you can grasp the significance of this observation. A pain occurs that we call pain or dislocation and instead of it being *nothing at all,* a nonevent we can take as a basis for hope, which would in some sense be God's *back,* it's a warning sign. Do you realize, Doctor, how serious it is that there can be no pain without a sequel? I'm circumcised, Doctor, my parents made it their duty to shield me from the laws of nature and I approve of this inheritance, symbolic though it be. So it's all the more difficult for me to concede that my body should be subject to the principle of causality. Still less the whole course of my life. Frankly speaking, the principle of causality revolts me. I put it to you, Doctor, if we suppose that my retina is not torn:

what's this medieval ankle boot doing at the center of my vision? You're stumped, Doctor. Ha ha ha! I gather you've not often come across the piked shoe in your books. Ha, ha, ha! What are you laughing at? says Marie Thérèse.

"Am I laughing?"

"Yes. We're here."

They've stopped in a little parking lot. The turn she's just made into the almost empty site suggests there's a space she always homes in on.

"Over there you have the Viry-Châtillon lake. It's very well known. People water-ski and sail there. There are ducks, swans."

"Do you water-ski?"

"No. I tried one year at Banyuls, I could never get started. That's where I live."

Marie-Thérèse points to a low, terraced apartment block that resembles certain vacation homes. There's not much around it, apart from a crane in front of a building under construction and another block set farther back. No more rain and fog. No more floating lights. No more warmth.

"Marie-Thérèse, take me back to Paris."

"Why, for goodness' sake?"

"Please."

"You're going to eat first, then we'll see. Come along."

Marie-Thérèse gets out of the car. Adam as well. Marie-Thérèse locks the doors. She says, "That's Grigny over there."

"I see."

"That's the public housing at Grande Borne."

"I see."

They stare at an illuminated hillside in the distance. Adam takes a few steps toward the lake. Marie-Thérèse follows him. Then they stop. After a moment Marie-Thérèse says, the area on the Grigny side is not so well looked after, they don't prune the trees, there are McDonald's wrappers. Adam nods. In silence they contemplate the low trees, the little hedges, the motionless water, the birds slipping along in the half-light. They contemplate the lampposts, the low-rise housing zone, the restaurant on the far shore. Marie-Thérèse is contemplating what she sees every day and every night. She's lost her energy, thinks Adam. He sees her in the bleak light, at last he can see her face, a somewhat sunken mouth, dark veins, nothing serious, just the passing of youth. Right, shall we go in? says Marie-Thérèse.

"So what's it like, that restaurant?"

"It's a restaurant."

"Do you go there sometimes?"

"No."

"Why?"

Marie-Thérèse shrugs her shoulders. Adam looks at the restaurant on the far shore. A white building with a green sign, the same green as the ankle boot, he thinks, and a balcony. Suppose we go there, he says.

"Oh no," she laughs.

"Why?"

"We haven't come here to go to a restaurant!"

"Why not?"

"I'm not going to a restaurant just down the road from me. If I go to a restaurant I go in Paris or somewhere else."

"But I'd very much like to go to that one."

"You'd be disappointed."

"Really?"

"It's dreary. And not very good."

"I see."

"And there's no one there in the evening."

"Oh," he says, staring at the tranquil building beside the water and thinking about the sad and childish and inexplicable desire to *go out to a restaurant*. One day when they were driving down south, at the start of Irène, he remembers, very long ago, they'd crossed deep valleys and reached a village on a hillside. The village was called Glandieu. At one end of a promenade of compacted earth there was a turn that vanished beneath a rock and at this spot there was a little restaurant. They'd sat down at a table outside and he'd said to himself, he remembers, I'm going to eat a good country terrine here and drink rough wine. I'll eat gherkins beneath a summer sun, while holding Irène's hand under the tablecloth. Can you hear the seagulls, can you see them? says Marie-Thérèse.

"I can see them."

At Saint-Vaast-la-Hougue he'd refused to rent bicycles. He recalls this stubbornness. Why had he refused to rent bicycles? The other families were cycling merrily along with the seagulls all around them. Fathers in shorts, mothers with knapsacks, cycling along amid the salt breezes and the cries of the gulls. What does this resistance signify? What ails a man who's afraid to rent bicycles? Yes, I can see the seagulls, Marie-Thérèse, and, though I don't understand what on earth they're doing in Viry-Châtillon, I can see them flying over this path for Sunday strollers and swooping down to the dull waters, I can see the lake, too, he thinks. I can see the lights of the life all around, Marie-Thérèse's summer house and Marie-Thérèse too, her coat, her scarf, her face of thirty years ago, I can see time has passed, I can see our old age under the white light of the street lamp, and when I don't want to look at anything and close my eyes I can see a piked shoe. At first, Doctor, I thought it was a car, you know, one of the long American ones. But now I remember those men in baggy trousers and long shoes on the squares in front of churches in my children's encyclopedia, I can see this teasing fluorescent green harbinger of death and it makes me think of our ancestors, I can understand all that, Doctor, I can picture all that, I can tell myself these are fragments of existence that I'm picturing, these are fragments of the universe I'm grasping, I can make links between the lake and the shadowy seagulls and the ducks, the restaurant and the curtains, I can imagine who lives up there in the housing development at Grigny, I can link my life and that of Marie-Thérèse, I can recall our life in Suresnes and imagine time as a climb up an immense, grievous, fatal staircase. My children, I can see them, too, in our apartment, I know what they're doing and I see their pajama-clad bodies. My wife, Irène, I can see too, even if I know nothing of her life. Even if I know nothing of her life. For I no longer know who she is and she doesn't know who I am. There are people I see three times a year whom I know better and who understand me better. When we go out she laughs, she goes into raptures, she takes umbrage, I simply don't understand this public animation, she never gives me secret looks—or only to reproach me for my absence—she never glances my way to convey one of those sweet, unspoken messages, I don't exist. She cheerfully makes jokes about us. The scientist and the poet, she dines out on that in company, her coarse banter disguises a gruesome pairing that she hasn't believed in for centuries, but without ever looking at me, I mean really looking at me and perceiving the extent to which this charade is painful to me. When we visit a place she makes idiotic comments in a voice that sets my teeth on edge, cultural observations she considers relevant that have no bearing on the actual facts of the case, in ringing tones that shatter the atmosphere, and if I say to her don't talk so loud or tell me later, or I don't give a damn, Irène, she gets on her high horse and falls into a silence so terrible there's no place else to go except the darkness of the crypt. I can see the book I shall never write, my unfulfilled dreams, I can see them, yes, Doctor, my unfulfilled dreams are like an archipelago within me, I can still just make it out, even though it's receding and its colors are fading, and it grows heavier and heavier within my body. I brought off *The Black Prince of Mea-Hor* because it's set outside the world, I can't picture the world. I can see only scattered fragments, shards, I can make no sense of it. I'm not capable of renting bicycles for my family because I'm simply not capable of grappling with *the idea of joy,* pedaling along amid the idea of joy kills me. Whistling along amid salt breezes with happy families is beyond my strength. If I get onto a bicycle with the little one on the saddle behind, what'll overcome me is the desire to weep. To avoid having the desire to weep, one would need to have made a success of everything else, to feel oneself in one camp or the other. Whistling along in single file with your wife and children amid the salt breezes is not the least you can do, it's the ultimate achievement. Yes, Marie-Thérèse, I can see the seagulls, they come from a long way off, tumbling over the little dunes and headlands. I can see them.

"Let's go in," says Marie-Thérèse.

He follows her. As she walks she jingles her keys. They make their way into the white apartment block. They make their way into the elevator. He sees himself in the mirror, holding the package from the pharmacy.

Marie-Thérèse opens the door to her apartment. She switches on the light. She hangs up her coat and scarf and says, Make yourself comfortable. She switches on a lamp on a low table that has an Oriental look. There's a sofa and an armchair, the floor is linoleum, Adam notes. At the end of the room a French door opens onto a balcony, beyond it the lake. Marie-Thérèse says, should I turn up the heat?

"If you like."

She goes into the kitchen and switches on the lights—it's a long, narrow room with a window at the far end. She turns on the boiler, tears off a paper towel, and blows her nose. Adam is still standing in the living room in his coat. We'll have a pick-me-up she says, opening a cupboard, a Pernod, a drop of cherry liqueur?

"OK. A drop of cherry liqueur."

Adam sits down in the armchair. Do I drink my Veinamitol before the cherry liqueur? he thinks. I'd have got it out of the way then, he thinks, but on the other hand, wouldn't the immediate intake of alcohol risk vitiating the effects of the Veinamitol? Shouldn't I leave a space between the Veinamitol and the alcohol, the way you're supposed to do with aspirin and antibiotics? Drink the cherry liqueur, he thinks, warm yourself up with the cherry liqueur and swallow your Veinamitol later, in a neutral context. Marie-Thérèse comes in with a tray on which there are glasses and a saucer of Tuc savory crackers. Take your coat off, she says, I've just turned up the heat! Unless, thinks Adam, I were to drink the Veinamitol right away and then eat a handful of crackers as filling before the cherry liqueur. Would you have a glass of water, Marie-Thérèse?

"Yes, if you take your coat off. It's all wet anyway."

Adam removes his coat. Marie-Thérèse goes to hang it up and returns with a glass of water. What's that? she says, watching him empty the packet into the glass.

"A thing for the circulation."

"You have a circulation problem?"

"It's not serious."

"Five drops of essential oil of garlic, plus two drops of lemon essence, three times a day."

"Really?"

"You can mix it with anything you like, honey, soft bread, or water."

"What does it do?"

"It regulates the circulation. It stabilizes hypertension."

"It acts on the blood vessels?"

"Of course."

"It strengthens them?"

"It strengthens everything."

Adam drinks the Veinamitol and takes a Tuc. Marie-Thérèse has gone off into the kitchen. She returns with a colander, some newspaper, and some potatoes. Adam eats the Tuc and she peels the potatoes, while taking sips of cherry liqueur. She's got no neck, he thinks, is it because she's all hunched over to do the peeling? Oh, my glasses! she exclaims, I'm forgetting my glasses. She laughs, getting up and rummaging in her bag. How do I look? Awful? A hundred years old?

"Not at all. Fine. They suit you fine."

"Goodness, I look a bit like Madame Demonpion!" she says, looking at herself in the hall mirror.

"Who's that?"

"Demonpion, our history and geography teacher."

"I don't remember her."

"Oh yes, you know, Demonpion: *plus ça change et plus c'est la même chose.*"

"I don't remember."

"Have you seen anyone again? Have you seen Tristan?" she asks, getting back to her peeling.

"I've not seen anyone."

"Neither have I, apart from Alice. And Tristan at the time of Alice's death. Since then I don't know what's become of him. At one time he had a kind of graphics outfit or something like that. Do you remember Gros-Dujarric? He did the Twingo campaign."

"I don't remember."

"He lived in the same building as Alice in the Hocquettes apartment complex. There were three of us in the class from the Hocquettes. I can see better with

these glasses, it's a shame to admit it but I can see better with these glasses. Do you want onions, would
you like me to add onions? I can make it with or without onions."

"Whatever you like."

"No, you tell me what you prefer."

"Add an onion."

"It improves it but there are people who don't like
onions. Do you cook?"

"Yes."

"What do you do that's good?" she says from a long
way off, peeling the onion under the tap at the sink.

"Pasta."

"What kind of pasta?"

"All kinds."

"Italian style?"

"Yes. I do risotto as well."

"I adore risotto. You must make me a risotto one
day."

"Yes."

She slices the potatoes, tosses the onion into a frying
pan, and returns to sit down facing him. And your
wife, does she cook? she says.

"Not a lot. She doesn't have time."

"What does she do?"

"She's an engineer."

"In what specialty?"

"Telecommunications."

Marie-Thérèse falls silent. She lowers her eyes and seems to be meditating on this reply. She polishes her spectacles with the cloth and puts them back in their case. The onion sizzles in the frying pan. She gets up to turn down the heat. She adds the potatoes, turns up the power in the exhaust fan, and leaves the kitchen, closing the door.

Marie-Thérèse and Adam sit facing each other. Without the background light from the kitchen the room has taken on the semblance of an empty space. On the low table, apart from the tray she's just brought in, there's a flower in a pot. When the daylight fades, Goncharki had said one day at his house, I don't get up to light the room. I don't switch on anything, I let things take on the semblance of shadows and if I'm doing something I continue doing what I was doing in the dark. Is it quiet in Viry? says Adam, after a long silence.

"Oh yes it's quiet," she says.

"What's it like?"

"Nothing much. Viry's neutral, it's not much of a place."

Help me, my God, he thinks, to transmute life into literature! To transmute Marie-Thérèse, the linoleum

floor, the Tucs, the gloomy light, to transmute Viry
and all the years into literature. I have no greater
wish. I offer up this prayer as I swallow a mouthful of
cherry liqueur: grant me the power to exist in spite of
and beyond reality. Until now I've not been sincere,
as you well know, I always wanted to be loved and
praised, I wanted to be *somebody,* my God. I've played
at being arrogant, a naysayer. What I wanted, and I
laugh at the phrase, was to occupy a place in our time.
Of all that I've written, the only thing I have any
affection for is *The Black Prince of Mea-Hor,* my one
book devoid of vanity. You see me tonight, seated
in this living room in Viry-Châtillon, observing the
configuration of the furniture, waiting with Marie-
Thérèse Lyoc for time to pass. A switched-off television on a television table: a combination you could
find in a hotel room. A set of shelves with CDs, a few
books and some photos on them, a sideboard adapted
to house hi-fi equipment, a Moroccan cushioned
footstool. A Bonnard picture on the wall, a reproduc-
tion on paper in a red frame. A woman pouring a cup
of tea for a dog that sits upright and obedient at the
table, waiting to be served. Here, where nothing is
happening, in the absence of any physical body, I feel
more disoriented than in the real world, which is, as I
heard a commentator on the radio put it, *in chemical*

precipitation. I think about my age and the seconds slip away into the void. Help me, God, to capture all this for the simple comfort of feeling I'm alive. Do you smoke? says Marie-Thérèse.

"No."

"Do you mind if I smoke? I hardly smoke at all during the day but in the evening I enjoy it."

"Go ahead."

The smoke spirals upward, shrouding the woman and her dog in a haze. In the past, he thinks, he's seen other works by Bonnard with a similar feel to them, or with animals in them, at any rate. The fading coil leaves a blurred impression. Adam suddenly sees coarse brushstrokes, a coarse palette, he tells himself, an excessive covering of the canvas, and he tells himself that he could suddenly no longer like Bonnard, he who'd always liked Bonnard, and that Bonnard, exhibited here on this ocher wall, by the light of this Oriental lamp, was turning out to be glutinous and messy, falsely cheerful. So one could always have liked Bonnard and suddenly no longer like him, so one could suddenly stop liking something, he thinks, stop liking a picture or a book or a place, stop liking anything at all, anyone at all, at one fell swoop. Five minutes ago you liked the painter Bonnard, he thinks, when your eyes lit upon this framed print you thought, look, Bonnard, and you liked the teapot, the composition, the dog, and the back of the chair and then all at once you no longer liked any of it at all, you loathed the woman, the dress, the wall, you found it all disgusting, you found it was a disgusting painting, you who a few minutes before and over long years had admired and liked the ingenuity, the warmth, the sensuality of Bonnard's paintings. The notion we form of things fades, he thinks. One day, he thinks, he must count the things he'd become disillusioned with. What are the masculine verbs? Goncharki had asked during one of their innumerable bibulous and elliptical discussions. Don't stop to think. Give me two. Holding and believing, Adam had replied. Isn't that your cell phone ringing? says Marie-Thérèse.

"Where is it?"

"I don't know, where was it?"

"In my coat."

"I hung it in the hall."

Adam runs into the hall. He thrusts his hand into one pocket, then the other, finally he takes out the cell phone: Hello, hello? he calls into the receiver in desperate tones. Hello? he says again, absurdly, into the silence. *Unknown caller* appears on the screen. Adam waits for the little envelope signifying a message to appear. He's standing in the hallway, between the kitchen and the living room. I take my coat, he thinks, I open the door softly, and I make my getaway. Were you too late? says Marie-Thérèse.

"Yes."

"They're better now, all the same. When cell phones started they'd ring only, oh three or four times, I don't remember now, you missed half the calls."

"That's right," he says, resuming his seat in the armchair.

"Would you like more Tucs?"

"No thanks."

The envelope doesn't appear. Adam dials his code. You have no new messages the voice tells him. She should shut her trap, that fat cow, he thinks, what right has the bitch to interfere in my life. Excuse me, Marie-Thérèse, I'm going to ring home just in case. "Maria, it's me. Did you call me just now?" "No." "Is everything OK, Maria?" "Everything's OK." "Irène hasn't got home yet?" "No." "Are the children in bed?" "They're going to bed." "They're not in bed yet?" "They're going to bed right now." "Tell Gabriel to use his electric toothbrush." "Fine." "And not to flood the bathroom the way he generally does." "Fine." "See you tomorrow, Maria." "See you tomorrow."

Maybe it was Albert, he thinks. I need to call my friend Albert, he says. It may have been him. "Hello?" "So?" says Albert. "Did you just call me?" "No. I've got better things to do, pal." "How's it going?" "Where are you?" "At Viry-Châtillon." "I hope it's worth the trip." "We're not talking about that category of event." "I see. So what category of event, then?" "Are you at Martine's?" "You can't talk?" "That's correct." "Ha, ha! You can't talk . . . !" "Right, I'm hanging up. *Ciao.*"

Who had been thinking of him at that late hour? What precious friend had wanted to make his voice heard? Save me, my friend, I wanted to talk to you, I ran but it was too late, ring again, save me. So does he flood the bathroom? says Marie-Thérèse.

"Excuse me?"

"Your son. You said tell him not to flood the bathroom."

"Yes. He floods the bathroom when he brushes his teeth."

"How?"

"He plays with the water in the sink. He makes waterfalls."

"Tell me about your children," says Marie-Thérèse, after a pause.

"What do you want to know?"

"Their ages, are they dark like you, although now, of course, you're . . ." She giggles.

"They're five and eight. They're dark."

"What grades are they in?"

"The younger one is in kindergarten, the older one is in second grade," he says, thinking, we're scraping the barrel here.

"Are they good students?"

"For heaven's sake, Marie-Thérèse."

"Here now, this is Andréas," she says enthusiastically, lifting a framed photograph off the shelf.

For a moment Adam cannot recall who Andréas is; when he sees the child's face he remembers the dentist. Andréas is in color, he's smiling. Can one call it a smile, this skewed twisting of the mouth? thinks Adam. The photographer has said to the child, come on, let's have a smile, and the child twisted his mouth sideways. Adam has already seen this expression on school-related portraits of his elder son, already seen the mindless, sickly pose against a background of cubes. He's already seen this woebegone face, he thinks, the long ears, the first communion haircut, already seen the part in his hair they'd sweated blood to create, the shirt buttoned too tightly, accentuating the puffy look, not, he knows, on his own child, but on the Adam Haberberg of long ago, and, as he holds the frame in his hand, not knowing what to do with it, he has to struggle against an unexpected impulse to burst into tears. After striving every day, he thinks, to rid oneself of compassion, advocating withdrawal and endurance as a way of life, when faced with the photo of a schoolboy one caves in. He didn't have his retainer by then, he says, for the sake of saying something. No, not yet, says Marie-Thérèse. But he was already an expert on dental occlusion, she adds proudly. He's apprehensive: she's not going to start on that again. But she doesn't start again, she puts the photo of Andréas back in its place and leaves the room. He hears her rummaging in another room at the end of the corridor then she returns holding something he recognizes as soon as he catches sight of it, which she places on his knees. Look, Demonpion, she exclaims, indicating the woman seated low down on the left in the front row. You. Alice. Serge. Tristan. Me. Corrine Poitevin. Blaise. Jenny Pozzo, she says. Philippe Gros-Dujarric. Evelyne Estivette. Hervé Cohen. Hervé Cohen, thinks Adam, looking at the grinning boy, I was friends with him. What happened to Hervé Cohen? he asks. I've no idea, says Marie-Thérèse. Adam remembers Hervé Cohen. A name vanished from his life, which he would never have uttered again but for this encounter. And yet he remembers Hervé Cohen, they used to go to each other's homes, they went on winter sports holidays in the Pyrenees. Adam remembers how they celebrated Passover in the hotel room at Font-Romeu. The Cohen parents were trying to locate Jerusalem. It's very simple, the father said, where's Perpignan? The mother pointed to one wall, he favored another, when did she have any sense of direction, he said, a woman incapable of opening the road map of France without homing in on Baden-Baden? In the end the father's geography won the day and they had, all of them, the parents, Hervé, his sister, Joëlle, and Adam himself, turned toward the wall opposite the window. During the prayer the mother had had a fit of the giggles, which spread to the children, while the father, in his jacquard ski pullover with the prayer shawl half flung over his head, continued to read the story of the Red Sea crossing earnestly and reprovingly to the bathroom door. The Cohen parents were the opposite of his own, thinks Adam. The Cohen parents were cheerful and irrational. The Cohen parents were marvelous. What counts, thirty years later, looking at this class photo, thinks Adam, is not Alice Canella, nor Tristan Mateo, nor Hervé Cohen, but the Cohen parents. Tristan, he notices, is wearing a white shirt, he has long hair and a mustache, a cross between Jim Morrison and Frank Zappa. Alice is slim, blond, sullen, as was fashionable at the time. Adam tries to picture her fat. And dead. Dead is easier, he thinks. At Font-Romeu the Cohen parents may well have been exactly my age now, he thinks. What's become of them? Dead, too? Or living somewhere, aged and shrunken. Or living somewhere, not aged and shrunken at all, looking after Hervé's and Joëlle's children, reciting the exodus from Egypt for the thousandth time, lighting candles at Hanukkah, railing against Israel, railing against the enemies of Israel, still bawling one another out over trifles, teasing one another. You could never have spoken of his own parents as the Haberberg parents the way you spoke of the Cohen parents. The Haberberg parents were austere and harassed and didn't love each other. They were not interested in their son's friends like the Cohen parents. Monsieur Cohen, Adam remembers, had taught him how to play "421," as well as the Hebrew alphabet and the rudiments of driving. He drove a Simca 1500 with the gearshift on the floor. For Father's Day Adam and Hervé had gone down to the car showrooms in the Avenue de la Grande Armée and bought him a wooden gearshift knob. This accessory had literally galvanized him, causing him to lurch from being a man known for his abrupt driving

into being a veritable public danger. In traffic jams
Cohen senior would *step on the gas* as soon as he had
ten yards clear in front of him. At every traffic light,
Adam recalls, they hurtled from the rear luggage
compartment to the windshield. Madame Cohen,
stoically, seemed to experience the untimely applica-
tion of the brake as an act of God. Adam had learned
to drive in the parking lot beside the Church of Stella
Matutina, a modern building Cohen said had been
designed by a great criminal. With Cohen as instructor, he and Hervé took turns as pupil and shaken pas-
senger. He used to say: look, my children, if I'd been
the architect of that church . . . I'd have begun by
building a synagogue! And he laughed at his own
joke, Adam remembered, the way he laughed when
we swerved, stalled, and had fits of panic. They won't
speak of Irène and me as the Haberberg parents
either, he thinks. No friend of his children is ever
going to remember them as *the Haberberg parents*. The
Haberberg parents don't give off anything. You felt
like a *son* with the Cohen parents.

"You've not changed at all, Marie-Thérèse," he says,
himself surprised at the truth of the statement.

"I'm better now. I looked like a country bumpkin."

"You looked like a country bumpkin but your face
hasn't changed."

"Neither has yours, very much, apart from your hair."

He has black, curly hair, he's slim, he's wearing a checked shirt. He thinks it's clever in the photo to be a rebel. He has a phony look about him. He's not very different from Serge Gautheron, of whom he has no recollection, but who has the same build, wears the same colors, and displays the same ridiculous arrogance. Quite the opposite of Tristan Mateo, he sees, who's a head taller than everyone else with a strikingly detached air in his flowing white California-style shirt. Tristan Mateo is reading Jim Morrison's *The Lords and the New Creatures,* he reads Herbert Marcuse and Jerry Rubin, smokes and imbibes all the substances of the period without ever feeling any the worse for it or flagging on the rugby field. Tristan Mateo owns Alice Canella. Alice Canella no longer exists, not for any of us, Adam tells himself, and the idea has a bitter and soothing savor. A barely perceptible savor, he observes, the tang of a fleeting mist instantly dissipated. Marie-Thérèse has gone to turn over the potatoes. Adam wonders where they will eat their supper. It must be possible for the two of them to sit together in the kitchen. Or else here, he supposes, at the low table. Adam can see no other table and concludes that Marie-Thérèse doesn't entertain her friends, or at least only one friend, or else friends who eat off their laps, sitting politely side by side, with their napkins and their plates on their tightly clenched knees. And he wonders who these friends are that come to eat dinner off their laps in Viry-Châtillon, in Marie-Thérèse Lyoc's neat and tidy apartment. And he concludes how lucky it is that such *living room* friends exist, whether in Orly now or Suresnes then, coming in at the main door, making their way into people's rooms with loud voices, instantly creating a good atmosphere, squeezing onto the sofa without any fuss, squabbling happily, laughing and knocking back the drinks. I could write about these Saturday friends, he thinks, after all, I know them, I see them flocking together like birds, I combine periods, I combine emotions, I shuffle lives like playing cards. Do you entertain friends here? he says.

"It depends," she replies from the kitchen, wiping her hands on the dishcloth. "Not all that much, in fact."

"You don't throw little dinner parties here from time to time?!"

"Not all that much. Would you like to eat in the kitchen or the living room?"

"Wherever you like."

"It's easier to sit in the kitchen."

"Fine."

"But the light's more pleasant in the living room."

"Whichever you prefer."

"You decide."

"It's all the same to me."

"Choose."

"In the kitchen," says Adam, and immediately thinks the living room would be better.

"It'll be ready in five minutes," she says, coming back to sit opposite him, and picking up her glass of cherry liqueur, content with the situation, it's hard to know exactly why. Adam has put the class photo on the table. Marie-Thérèse picks it up and pores over it. She knows that photo by heart, thinks Adam, that class photo has traveled through the years like her face, changing imperceptibly, receding in time, he tells himself. She's uncovering a whole carnival of ghosts, this evening, poor thing, he thinks, as she sits there unexpectedly face-to-face with the bald, paunchy old man they used to call Adam Haberberg. He remembers the name in its youth, he remembers how Adam Haberberg used to have quite a different ring to it, it didn't mean what it says today. Unlike Marie-Thérèse Lyoc, he thinks. Marie-Thérèse Lyoc has always meant Marie-Thérèse Lyoc. Marie-Thérèse Lyoc is definitive, he thinks. Not Adam Haberberg. It was a name you could count on, it was, in fact, the only thing his parents had given him that could be counted on. When you're called Adam Haberberg you don't expect to write pulp fiction and you don't expect to be laid low by thrombosis at the age of forty-seven before any *recognition,* however small, however hybrid, however fatally ephemeral, has occurred. Adam always thought his career had, inexplicably, got off on the wrong foot. To win at "421," Cohen had instructed him, you have to want to win. If you leave it to fate, the dice can sense it, they're not motivated. Cohen won every time. Adam would warm the dice in his hand, blow on them, call out the numbers in advance in a resolute voice and lose. The dice responded to the silent will, not the antics of a yappy little dog. Did things go the same way in life? Does life respond to the silent, unspoken will, which is not only the will but the certainty that the world is on offer and isn't going to go on its way without you. For to win, he'd learned you don't need to want to win, you need to believe you will win. Holding and believing, he remembers replying to Goncharki without stopping to think, the masculine verbs. Without stopping to think, he muses, which doesn't mean without lying, it would be wrong to confuse spontaneity with truth, he tells himself. To survive, he thinks, one has had to construct postures conducive to self-respect. You can't say I haven't changed at all, says Marie-Thérèse. Then she adds, there's something I want to show you. But she doesn't stir. What? says Adam.

"A letter."

"A letter from whom?"

"From Alice."

Adam is silent and Marie-Thérèse doesn't stir. They remain thus, unmoving, and finally Marie-Thérèse says, yesterday at a crossroads, on the Boulevard Sébastopol, I was waiting with some other people to cross. At a given moment there were no cars either to the left or to the right and the light was still green. Everyone crossed except me. Even when I could still have done it, I didn't, I don't know why, I waited all alone on the sidewalk till the light turned red. Adam expects something more but there's nothing more. Marie-Thérèse has finished. They fall silent again and then Marie-Thérèse says, that's how it is in life, I don't dare, I'm too law-abiding. Now I'm putting the eggs in.

She gets up, goes back into the kitchen. He sees her pouring the beaten eggs into the frying pan and going through the actions of the omelette. Adam gets up and joins her. The kitchen is long and narrow; he goes up to the window at the end. In the darkness, several bare trees, buildings with no windows, lampposts, tiers of seats. What's that you can see? he says.

"The football stadium."

"And the road beyond, what's that?"

"That's the road leading from Route Nationale 7 to the throughway."

"Can I do something?"

"You can uncork the wine. Would you like salad?"

"Fine."

"Sit down."

Adam sits down. He's thinking about the letter. Don't say what was that letter from Alice? he tells himself.

"Do you ever meet up with Serge Gautheron?"

"No. He's remarried."

"I see."

"He has a son."

"Shall I give you some wine?"

"Go ahead."

"What was that letter from Alice?"

"I'll show it to you."

"I really don't care. So what was it?"

"You'll see."

Marie-Thérèse slides the omelette onto a round dish, which she sets between them on the narrow table. It's a beautiful potato omelette, well folded, moist, a perfect omelette, thinks Adam. Imagine, if someone had said to me this morning, tonight you'll be dining here with Adam Haberberg! She laughs as she serves him. On the counter along the wall, there's a lineup of appliances. A kettle, a juicer, notes Adam, a blender, a mixer, an electric coffeemaker, a toaster. Adam closes his eyes. The green fluorescent piked shoe is there, confirming the supremacy of solitude. Do you use all these machines? he says. Oh yes, she lights up in an unexpected way, yes, less than in the old days, of course, but I certainly do.

"What do you make?"

"Everything." She laughs. "Last weekend, for example, I made four zucchini loaves for my sister's twenty-fifth wedding anniversary."

"I see."

"When I say I made them, it's the machines that do it, I do nothing. Is it good? Add a little salt if you want."

"It's very good."

"Some women are crazy about shoes or beauty products, me, I'm crazy about electrical appliances. When I got my first washing machine early in my marriage, we'd never had one for want of space, I switched on the long-wash program. I sat beside it on a stool and watched the whole process, prewash, wash, starching, spinning . . . up to the final click. I learned all the sounds by heart. These days I can detect the slightest suspicious sound. The same for the dishwasher. When I open a magazine I don't look at fashion or gossip, I look at 'What's New?' in the household electricals section. I'm very choosy, either it's love at first sight and I'm round at the store the next day, or I wait for years before making up my mind in the hope of a better performance or a new image. The image is very important, I'm in a good position to know this, being in business myself. Once I've decided on an appliance I'm quite capable of hitting the roof if they don't have the color I want. My kitchen is my home, I like to be the boss in my kitchen, making all my appliances toe the line gives me a buzz. I read the instructions thoroughly, a set of instructions in too many languages infuriates me, and what's more it's always the French that comes last. Instructions that don't explain enough irritate me as well, lots of things irritate me, for instance I had a blender that would make juice but you had to add an extra gadget and keep it on the top, I like it when the machine works all by itself. I made four zucchini loaves last weekend, do you know how long it took me? A quarter of an hour. I wash the zucchini, I chop the ends off—I also have the correct knives for this, even for a trivial little recipe—I set up the KitchenAid with the attachment for round slices,

I select the cutter for medium slices, neither too thin nor too thick. The slices fall into the big container, five or six at a time, you have to keep pace with the machine, I don't want to stop it, it's a battle, between it and me. When the pot's full I always feel it's a miracle, I add olive oil, basil—I don't use a spoon, I use my hands, I've picked that up from American TV serials, American women use their hands—salt, pepper, the best chili pepper, I knead it, I put it on one side, I take my blender, put in my crème fraîche, my eggs, I add some tarragon, I mix everything together. I oil my baking tins a little, put several slices in the bottom and a sprig of basil to decorate it, when it's fully mixed, I taste it, I pour in the mixture and put it into the oven that's already preheated. It takes me a mere fifteen minutes and I've almost nothing to do. Every evening I set the time for my coffee. When I get up the first thing I can smell is the aroma. Really fresh, hot coffee, measured and blended to perfection. That's what's so wonderful, it's as if someone had been taking care of you while you were asleep and then discreetly gone away."

"Yes," murmurs Adam.

"I'm going to make a salad," she says, getting up. "A tomato salad, would that suit?"

Adam acquiesces and while the idea of living in a log

cabin in Canada with nothing but an ax lingers and fades, he wonders whether he, too, wouldn't like to get up to the smell of coffee, wonders whether it wouldn't be better to be alone like Marie-Thérèse with the Krups coffee machine rather than alone at the ravaged breakfast table in the morning, facing Irène's teapot, the emptied bowls of chocolate, the Cap'n Crunch box, the half-eaten pieces of toast, without any visible sign of attention to his own existence other than a cup and saucer taken out of the cupboard and set down any old where. Marie-Thérèse has sliced the tomatoes with one of her special knives, and as she stirs the salad dressing in the bowl Adam notices her bosom quivering. The quivering of Marie-Thérèse's bosom inexplicably evokes a certain mountain climate, the opaque and shifting humidity of trails of mist, as if life should resolve itself into a single bleak image. The bleak rain or these billowing breasts in the long, narrow kitchen, beyond which the future lies hidden.

She has resumed her seat and put the salad bowl on the table between them, and smiles at him. He responds, as he had done in front of the big cats' house, to this silent signal. He watches her mixing the tomatoes, serving him delicately. She cuts some bread, it's bread with a bit of brioche flavor, it's Andréas's bread, she says, he loves it, I always have some in the house, I freeze it. He sees them, her and him, sitting at table in the long, narrow kitchen, poised between the lake of Viry-Châtillon and Route Nationale 7, he thinks of men sitting at tables in long, narrow kitchens, amid the wilderness of the cities, eating a tomato salad, an omelette, or anything quite ordinary, and thinks help me, my God, to find the words. I'll be happy to write pulp fiction to earn my living, I don't see anything wrong in earning my living by calling myself Jeffrey Lord or Michael Brice, I'll be happy to forge ahead into the dark with my voyager through infinite space or, like Goncharki, with cops who never fuck for less than six hours at a stretch, I'll be happy to write *machine gun* for the guy going back to barracks, I'll be happy in future to write *a shiver ran down his spine,* I don't give a damn. Just grant me a secret notebook and help me to find the words to tell the truth. The medicines, the terror of decline, the food processor, Marie-Thérèse's jeans, the square of window at the end with the flapping awning. The truth with no wish, no desire for originality, without any desire at all. It doesn't matter if I'm a loser. In the morning I listen to the unstoppable radio getting excited about the great changes happening in the world and I think, you too should get excited, for heaven's sake, about the great changes happening in the world, that's what's expected of a writer, he should take note of History's fallout. But I no longer see any subject matter in the great changes happening in the world. I used to think I could when I was bonding with the prevailing culture, I don't anymore. The great changes happening in the world don't make any difference to what I am. At best they distract me from myself. Events are like the opium of forgetfulness, when I'm alone in the morning I switch on the appalling radio so as to be engulfed by events. Great events console me, they serve as alibis for my obscurity, you can't compete with global tragedy. Great events help to pass the time, nothing more. In my secret notebook I want to give an account of what doesn't change, or changes very little, or changes in an invisible, secretly cruel way. It doesn't matter if I'm a loser. My word, you were hungry, says Marie-Thérèse.

"It's true, he admits, "I was cold and hungry. You gathered up a piece of flotsam, Marie-Thérèse."

She's on her feet, she takes several cheeses out of the refrigerator and arranges them on a small tray. They don't look terrific but they're good, she says. After that I have fruit or a raspberry sorbet. Shall I open another bottle?

"Fine. Flotsam that I am, I'll try to keep my end up."

"What were you doing at the menagerie?"

"Nothing."

"It's a bit odd, all the same. In this weather."

"What's that?"

"It's chabichou. Goat."

"So, this letter from Alice."

"After dinner."

"Why did you divorce?"

"Because it wasn't working anymore. Why do people divorce?"

"It takes more than that."

"It's a good reason all the same."

"What wasn't working anymore?"

Marie-Thérèse pauses to think. Then she says: we didn't love each other anymore.

"And to begin with you did love each other?"

"I think so."

"You're not sure."

"Yes, I am."

"Why did you say I think so?"

"If you'd like a sorbet I'll take it out now."

"No sorbet."

Marie-Thérèse gets up and puts the basket of fruit on

the table. Winter fruits, apples, a pear, oranges. In her house, he thinks, she has everything she needs to welcome any unexpected visitor, she who never entertains anyone, or hardly ever, she said, can offer a plain meal at the drop of a hat, a basic gesture, he thinks, of which he would never have been capable at any time in his life, since it calls for a domestic order to reign within the house, which, in the hierarchy of types of order, is geared to time and feast days—and there was never any house where this was the case. Even as a married man, even as a *paterfamilias,* he thinks, I've always lived with more or less empty cupboards, or at least only pasta and rice and boxes of instant mashed potatoes, with the refrigerator more or less empty, if you exclude the mountains of children's desserts, a refrigerator crammed to excess from time to time and then quickly emptied for an indefinite period, although it contains the basic necessities, bought at random by Irène, Maria, or myself, simply to provide for the needs of the day, it's a house which is the opposite of that imaginary house with its ever open door, where the table is laid for whoever enters, where the prophet Elijah may well come in one day, sit down, and drink his glass of wine. Your ocular tension is nineteen, the optometrist said, which, precisely speaking, is not a significant tension, but nor is it an anodyne one, I have patients who can go up to thirty-five, to give you an order of magnitude, or even fifty in certain extreme cases, on the other hand ocular tension varies, we need to control it before we have to worry about it, there are glaucomas where there's no tension, this does occur, but it's quite rare, in general a glaucoma translates into an increase of tension, though there are glaucomas where there's no increase of tension, in your case, where the optic nerve emerges at the base of the eye you present a papillary excavation, Adam remembers the optometrist saying, after he has suddenly felt an external bilateral pressure bearing down on both eyeballs, while watching Marie-Thérèse wrapping the cheeses up again in silver foil. A pressure of a completely different nature from the phenomenon of dislocation, he concludes, the latter, he now realizes, having so to speak disappeared, leaving behind as a memento the silent and terrifying shape of the piked shoe. So we should have two distinct effects, he thinks, to support the hypothesis of the two distinct and concomitant causes, thrombosis and glaucoma. Thus, he muses, maybe I do have glaucoma as well, since there's a thrombosis, why shouldn't there be glaucoma as well, he muses, as soon as one disorder appears, you look for other disorders, lurking there in the shadows, like our obsessions, with lives of their own, impelling each of us separately toward catastrophe. I must telephone the lab and get an earlier visual field test, thinks Adam. Why should I wait another fortnight to confirm a diagnosis I can already make here in the kitchen in Viry, as I watch Marie-Thérèse closing the cheese box, not even knowing whether these are the last images my brain will ever record with clarity, the last well-defined images of my life, Marie-Thérèse Lyoc in her long, narrow kitchen, the apples, the oranges, the crenelated dessert plates. He remembers the ostriches at the Jardin des Plantes. They're far away now, he tells himself, ostriches observed a few hours earlier already belong to the past. I feel nostalgia for that pair of ostriches, for the enclosure, the bench, the rain, I feel nostalgia for the patinated lion towering above the fountain, for the Rue Cuvier, for the Quai Saint-Bernard, the Marie-Thérèse who came toward me with her bags of samples and her umbrella is already in the past. Once they'd crossed the Paris beltway, he remembers, a sense of something irreparable had overcome him. Once they'd left the Boulevard Kellermann behind, at the first road sign for Montrouge, he'd felt irreparably lost, that was how it had struck him in the Jeep Wrangler. You have, Doctor, the privilege of receiving in your consulting room a patient of forty-seven who presents a double risk of blindness. This patient, Doctor, you should know, lacks courage. He makes you believe in his courage, especially by his penchant for assimilating your scientific terms, but he has none. He's an ordinary man who dreads failing health and being blind. Who dreads having to renounce what he's never had. Take the pear, says Marie-Thérèse.

"No thank you."

"Well, an apple then."

"Fine."

"All right?"

"Yes."

"Does the light trouble you?"

"No."

"I'll switch off the ceiling light, if you like."

"It's nothing, Marie-Thérèse."

She's already stood up. She presses the switch to the left of the door. The neon ceiling light and a wall spotlight go out. All that remains is the light on the exhaust fan and the strip lights that illuminate the counter, an absurdly intimate atmosphere that, when she asked, he approved, for, he observes, he can find no reason to resist her action, if she wanted to plunge the entire kitchen into darkness he wouldn't perceive it as inconvenient, he has no opinion, as well the glare of the neon as darkness, he thinks, as well words spoken as fruit cut up in silence. He has said, it's nothing, Marie-Thérèse, and she has gotten up to switch off the ceiling light, a pointless gesture, since he's not troubled by the light, a misguided solicitude, that both touches and irritates him. Instead of saying, It's nothing, Marie-Thérèse, why not admit everything, and even lay it on a bit thick to alarm her, what's the point of holding things back with this phony decorum that's already been undermined by his knitted brow, the Veinamitol, and his pathetic hand pressed to his eyelids, why not create a bit of atmosphere and say, Marie-Thérèse I have a serious genetic defect, at any moment, in any part of my body, one of the blood vessels could become blocked, even as I speak, I already have a thrombosis of the eye that is complicated by glaucoma, it might occur in my heart or in my brain, before the end of our evening together I could, for example, be struck down by a heart attack, and whether you switch your ceiling light on or off, Marie-Thérèse, makes no difference. The same goes for your essential oils, my poor Marie-Thérèse. I bear you no ill will but I hope you can gauge how ridiculous it was to recommend oil of garlic to me. Oil of garlic to a man with *hyperhomocysteinemia!* My wife, Irène, also urges miraculous brews on me. In her case not from ignorance, but from malice. Internal lotions for the venous system, prescribed by the girl who waxes her legs. Irène cannot tolerate my whining. She's the one who talks about *my* whining. As if I whined all the time, which isn't true, or which may have become true owing to the fact that, never having known the solace of any kind of tolerance in her, I've ended up emphasizing my complaints, even dramatizing them, in the paradoxical hope of being taken seriously, of melting the other, arousing her compassion. It's true that with my wife, Irène, I exaggerate my suffering and in a general way always have done, whatever my ills were, but I did it to attract her to me and that was a great mistake, Marie-Thérèse, because suffering cannot be communicated, any more than the sense of rejection, which is also called loneliness, can be, any more, which is worse, than grief can be, indeed I'm forced to wonder what can be communicated. Until now I've never had anything serious. All kinds of ills, yes. More or less everyday ills, yes. But nothing serious. I didn't tell you in the Wrangler, Marie-Thérèse, but my father had cancer of the colon. A cancer of a hereditary type, apparently. I'd come to accept the idea of cancer of the colon. My hypothetical worst case, since you need to have one, was the colon. The day I had a polyp-free colonoscopy I told myself, you're in the clear, nothing can happen to you. A little colonoscopy once every five years and you've nothing to worry about. One morning, Marie-Thérèse, I wake up, I have a flickering sensation in my left eye, I cover the other eye with my hand, and I become aware that my vision's blurred. I say to Irène my vision's blurred, she replies that's all we needed. I say to Irène the sight in my left eye's all hazy, she replies it's a speck of dust, it'll pass. Two days later I tell her I have a thrombosis, she sighs and says that's the last straw. The beautician's lotion is a thick, revolting concoction with a base of virgin vine, concentrated silica, and, I read on the label, because whereas you read instructions for electrical household appliances from start to finish, Marie-Thérèse, I read the labels on medicines from start to finish, of *witch hazel*. Witch hazel? I timidly dared to ask a woman who is, after all, a project leader at Issy-les-Moulineaux, a space communications buff. Witch hazel, that's right, she replies with an impatient shrug. You've swallowed far worse in your life. Where was I, Marie-Thérèse? What was I saying? You're lighting a candle on the table, we've gone back into the living room, I see, I'll go wherever you want, I'll sit wherever you want, the kitchen, the living room, it doesn't matter. The pathways I love, the trails that twist and turn who knows where, are far away.

Marie-Thérèse lights a white candle like an altar candle. From the flame she lights her cigarette. Then she says, do you want to see Alice's letter? Adam watches the thread of black smoke disappearing. He says, show me. Marie-Thérèse lays her cigarette down on a trefoil-shaped ashtray and goes off to fetch the letter.

Alice's letter is addressed to Marie-Thérèse Lyoc, Domaine des Hocquettes, Suresnes 92, Francia. Barely legible over the Spanish stamps, the postmark reads 1971.

Adam takes the sheets of paper out of the envelope. Four pages, covered right up to the edges in handwriting that is instantly recognizable and instantly painful.

MALAGA, SATURDAY AUGUST 14

Mujer (my burden!),

There's never any paper at all in the shithouses in Spain or Morocco, it's still as disgusting as ever and even though you wrote to me on some kind of toilet paper, which was a relief because I thought you were turning bourgeois, I don't use it despite my catching dysentery in the south of Morocco! I've got the cramps and heartburn, etc., it's such a "pain in the ass" that for the past four days I've stopped smoking . . . cigarettes. I'm here at the station, on the way back to Paris, a lot of hesitating, as I wanted to stay with Nordine at Diabet (a mile and a half from Essaouira, look on the map, dear). You can live on nothing down there, it's a village where the only people are hippies and Moroccans, but they're not stupid pricks, they take no notice of the hippies, don't regard them as strange animals the way people do everywhere else. Not a single tourist, it's really paradise. My parents would never have been able to find me down there, impossible. When I got here I found a letter from my father that starts like this: "The little notice you take of us speaks volumes for your inability to fulfill your most basic obligations. Am I to assume that you take a similarly casual view of your examination at the start of the new term and, beyond that, the year ahead? I must remind you that there's more to life than running after guitar-strumming morons on the beaches of the Costa del Sol." You can see what that kind of language does for one's morale! The truth is I find it hard to see myself going back to the lycée. To begin with, I've forgotten everything, absolutely everything, and, besides, for the past three weeks I've been stoned, this is the first day I haven't smoked, not taken my little dose of brain vitamins. You know ghita tea, opium tea? In Morocco everyone's high, even the customs men smoke, you smoke with the policemen, who are great, out in the street, in the cafés,

everywhere, you never hide and it costs nothing. For seven
francs you can get a pound of very good kif. The truth is I
can't see myself remaining in Suresnes. Nordine wants to
come and meet up with me after working in San Sebastian
for a month and we'll go off to Amsterdam where he's got
something fixed up. He wants us to get married, have a son,
and travel. He's very nice, I like him. I've even talked to
him about Tristan and also Julio, who's waiting for me in
Madrid to go off to Argentina and do craft work there. He
wants a son, too, it's an obsession, I don't know what's got
into them, that they all want a son (apart from Tristan). I
need to make my mind up once and for all which of them is
the best for me, and stay with him and forget all the others
because things can't go on like this (at the moment it's going
fine).

[SUNDAY 15 (8:30 A.M., SNIFF-SNIFF)]
Here we go! I told Nordine I wasn't going to stay in Madrid
but I thought it was too ridiculous, after Julio and me
writing rubbish to each other for a year not to go and see him
and I went, a bit reluctantly and it was the big
WHAMMO, all over again. We were together from
10:00 p.m. to 8:00 a.m. I've just left him, he was weeping,
it's stupid to play at ghosts, we really love each other! I think
I'm going to go off to Argentina with him. Of course there's

the question of cash. I'll do all I can to get some, I'll make necklaces with the stones from Mauritania I bought, I'll sell everything, you'll help me, I hope, my love, maybe I'll do fashion photos, at the moment I'm a bit of a walking skeleton. I'll look after children (not mine, I hope, I forgot to take the pill once, I was stoned, I took it next morning), I'll take my exam in the fall, behave extra normally at home, pile up the cash and one day disappear. They won't come looking for me in Argentina! Two things are a pain in the ass, leaving my burden (you) and then Tristan. I don't know how I'll react when I see him again, I think I really want to make him suffer. I've bought some hookahs and some pipes, I haven't smoked for two days now but my pupils refuse to go back to normal. There I go, ranting on, my love, I'm sorry, all I'm doing is talking about myself but it does me good to get it off my chest, I'm afraid you're always the one who catches it. To answer your question: Adam Haberberg may have been in love with me, like half the boys in the lycée (no false modesty, girl!!!) but first of all, let me reassure you, he's not my type at all, too transparent! You're the one who interests him now, I'm sure. Get your little brain working: Why do you think he walked home with us after the party at Meudon? If it had been for my sake he wouldn't have walked me home first and you second. If he walked you home second it was to be alone with you. He's in love with you but he's shy, you're pathetically shy, the pair of

*you. Instead of stupidly crying your eyes out every night
when you think of him, make the first move, girl! What's
the risk? You're well matched, he's nice, he's good-looking,
you'll always have plenty of time to meet sons of bitches, the
streets are full of them, and when some son of a bitch takes
your virginity, you'll say, "Oh! Where have all the nice
guys like Adam gone!" Write me a long letter to Suresnes,
I'm going to be alone and the chances are I won't be feeling
too great when I get back, especially if I've no cash for the
vitamins a girl needs for her peace of mind. We're just
coming to the frontier, I'll try to mail this letter if there's a
box. I'm sending this to you at Hocquettes, I've lost your
address in Cavalaire-sur-Mer, I hope they forward it. Have
fun, my love. Do lots of bathing and if you see something
nice, buy it for me.*

Alice. V peace to you.

Adam folds up the pages. He slides them under the
envelope without looking up. The Spanish stamps
depict a mournful man dressed in black with a white
collar against a black background. Each worth four
pesetas.

Marie-Thérèse sits bolt upright on the sofa, smoking
yet another cigarette, he thinks, since the previous
one couldn't have lasted that long. They can hear the
awning tapping outside the window. One of life's

trivial sounds, he thinks, but nothing's trivial right now, he tells himself, as the revelation of an utterly dead past mingles with a devastating confession. If he'd been in a different mood he could have laughed it off (though no one laughs lightly here in the funeral vault of Viry-Châtillon). And if he'd been in a different mood he would have heard nothing melancholy in the rattling of the awning. He's read these pages without suffering any shock, he tells himself. If the past is now turning into this incoherent hubbub, the present is destined for the same fate. Is it the essence of time sooner or later to be nothing more than an incoherent hubbub? Turned to stone in front of her altar candle, Marie-Thérèse pays no heed to these sterile questionings, she's triggered her device and now she waits. But what are you waiting for, Marie-Thérèse, you who up until now seemed literally inoffensive? You've kept this letter for more than thirty years. Could you know that one night of madness I'd come and collapse in your mortuary? In a different mood I'd be laughing about it, as I'll laugh tomorrow with Albert. I'd remark casually and with a mocking air, So, Marie-Thérèse, is that how it was, did I haunt your nights? Tomorrow I'll have a good laugh with Albert. Provided I leave here unharmed, provided I can negotiate what comes next with intelligence. The pressure on his eyes has now spread right across his face. Adam approves the giant hand pressing down on his temples, the center of his forehead, his cheek-bones. That the pain should abandon the fateful territory of his eyes is a victory in itself, he thinks. But why must my body sanction such a completely irrational anguish? In a different mood I wouldn't take a tragic view of an unfortunate development. But I'm not in a different mood. I'm in a mood to take a tragic view of any barrier to my peace of mind. Is it reasonable to blame someone for his mood? To Irène, who is constantly critical of all his ups and downs, he had declared, I see nothing in the constituent elements of a man more philosophical than his mood. What you call contradictions, Irène, are simply changes of perspective. I know I was the one, he'd said, who proposed Saint-Vaast-la-Hougue, thinking forty-eight hours with all four of us by the seaside, that's within the reach of any ordinary family, and I reproached you for doing the packing halfheartedly, I reproached you for not seeming happy to be going off with your husband and children to eat seafood on the Cotentin, I said if your family pisses you off you shouldn't have embarked on this adventure, I probably said it in less well chosen words, I no longer recall, I said when you have a family you have to accept the constraints. At Saint-Vaast-la-Hougue I didn't want to rent bicycles, I criticized the town, the sea, the people, the prices, I criticized the children's upbringing, everywhere I pulled a dour face, you said no one wanted this weekend, it was entirely your idea and you displayed such freakish energy in making it happen, you're the one that dragged us into this nightmare thanks to your sudden faith in harmony, your inexplicable and furious desire for harmony. Irène, at the moment when I'm saying let's go to Saint-Vaast-la-Hougue, I really believed that joy is possible in Saint-Vaast-la-Hougue, we've hardly gotten onto the staircase with the suitcases when I know no joy is possible in Saint-Vaast-la-Hougue or anywhere else, in the car I bounce back again. I create a good atmosphere, I deliver a lecture on the tides, I say we're going to see seagulls, I say we're going to collect seashells, which is, in fact, the last thing in the world that interests me, I could never give a damn about seashells, seashells never meant anything to me but I sincerely believe we can suddenly make friends with seashells, I sing old chart-toppers and put on funny voices to make people laugh, I buy a water pistol, which you disapprove of and you're right, the water pistol is a stupidity, and we stop talking and we're all unhappy in the car as it continues heading for God knows where. Maybe one day, Irène, I'll no longer believe that joy is possible in Saint-Vaast-la-Hougue or anywhere else, it'll be no to everything in advance, you'll no longer have to suffer from my moods, there'll be no more doomed departures. The sphinx Lyoc has stubbed out her cigarette. When Adam finally looks at her she's taken off her sneakers and stretched out her legs on the sofa. He still has the envelope and the pages of the letter in his hand. What does she expect? Why did she show him that letter? A woman who doesn't dare cross an empty boulevard with the other pedestrians. What's the significance of this silence and this somewhat languid posture? On top of the thrombosis, the Cotentin, the disaster of his book, did he need Marie-Thérèse Lyoc as a hetaera in Viry-Châtillon? She's left a blue night-light on in the kitchen. The way things are going, he thinks, trapped between the autopsy room and the darkness of the lake, I am being *called upon* to respond to a fantasy from thirty years ago. Tomorrow Albert and I will laugh. For an instant the possibility of an embrace crosses his mind. He studies Marie-Thérèse for the first time and notes that, by the flickering light of the altar candle, doubtless enhanced by the oblique backlighting, she has the hint, he thinks, not of a mustache but a goatee. He notices the shoulders, towering above the Albertian bosom, abnormally vigorous shoulders. She's strong, he says to himself, she's a crusher. I must confess my thrombosis to her. The thrombosis is a valid reason for not going the whole hog. I'm afraid it's no good your hoping for me to be physically compliant and available, Marie-Thérèse. . . . What if she doesn't understand what I'm driving at? Or pretends not to understand? You can't go in like a bull at a gate. Women want preliminaries. They want to hear words, declarations, declarations of weakness if need be, of uncertainty, of impotence, any old declaration. You thought you were safe from life here in this hideaway in Viry. You didn't foresee life effecting an entry through who knows which door, and compelling you to negotiate, not some carnal and in any case physically impossible issue, nor the resultant humiliation to which you attach no importance, but a lurch toward pity. Pity, he thinks, directed just as much toward Marie-Thérèse as to himself, a funereal pity, reaching out toward the light, to objects, to the cold edges of the walls. A pity, he knows, which he could make use of right now, and which would in some sense be the only valid argument for writing, but which, failing a miracle, he will not, he believes, have either the time or the strength to exploit. It's all happening too late, he thinks. And it all comes down to the same thing. To have been Adam Haberberg or Marie-Thérèse Lyoc, the faces in black and white in the school yard at Suresnes, the faces now lying there on the table in a row, kept apart by everything in the old days, it all comes back to the same thing. Little by little, he thinks, what we took for reality proves to be an illusion, name, work, the future. Outside the window he hears the gulls crying. Cries from far away arriving to underline the unreal and aberrant silence that must, he thinks, be broken at all costs. How am I going to get home? A taxi? In Viry-Châtillon after dark? It would be better to fake an apoplectic fit and call an ambulance. But it's Marie-Thérèse who stirs. She gets up and walks around the low table. When she reaches him she seizes the pages of the letter and holds them to the candle flame. What on earth are you doing! cries Adam, getting up at once and grasping the pages to save them. Marie-Thérèse hangs on. Stop, Marie-Thérèse, it's idiotic!

"What's it to you?" she says, pushing away Adam's hands and clinging firmly to the bundle. Adam fights back, drags at the paper and gathers up the torn fragments. It makes no sense, Marie-Thérèse! he implores, mesmerized by her frenzied action.

"It makes no sense to keep this letter."

"You've kept it for thirty years."

Marie-Thérèse tries to take back the rest of the letter. Adam screws the sheets into a ball and hides them behind his back.

"Give it to me."

"No."

Adam dodges Marie-Thérèse's hands. Was she vexed by his lack of reaction? Vexed by his silence, the unhappy woman now wants to destroy all trace of her past error. To burn her shame, he thinks as he uses the armchair as a shield, and sizes up the inexplicable puerility of his own behavior. They make several feints around the armchair, then Adam escapes toward the window. Come on, give it to me! She laughs, waltzing around him. Give it to me, laughing her incongruous throaty laugh. Marie-Thérèse laughs. This is how great love affairs begin. People spinning around each other laughing. The lover holding the parcel and the coquette spinning this way and that, trying to grab it. Granted, the drama is not generally played out in the morgue at Viry-Châtillon, the principals are not fifty-year-olds, don't have thrombosis, don't sell merchandise. But no matter. This is a variation. Adam passes the ball of paper from one hand to the other, raises his arms, Marie-Thérèse hops around chuckling, without her sneakers she's just a little shorter than him. She has abandoned all restraint, her face is pure toothy glee, foolish rapture, he thinks. He surprises himself in several physical pranks, feints, wrong-footings, high throws, the ball flies, disappears. At a given moment Adam miscalculates his lunge and inadvertently throws it across the room. The ball lands on the top of the sideboard. Both rush for it. Adam bangs into the corner of the low table, Marie-Thérèse grasps the tattered scraps. Got it! she cries. Got it! she sings, letting the pages flutter past her eyes as she unfolds them and Alice Canella's coarse blue handwriting, crossed out in places, reappears on them. Adam has collapsed onto the sofa. He's hurt his knee and the pain in his forehead has invaded new territory, he notes, it's now reached his nose and upper jaw. On the bookshelf Andréas smiles crookedly in his silver frame. Maybe I should consult a dentist as well, thinks Adam. Marie-Thérèse glances through the smoothed-out fragments of the letter in silence. She thrusts the pages at the candle and lays down the little torch on the trefoil-shaped ashtray. There's a mild blaze, the pages stretch out and curl up, there are flames, smoke, a lingering bluish glow, and then a blackened mass.

"I thought it would make you laugh," says Marie-Thérèse as the acrid smell fades.

"What?"

"The letter. I thought it would make you laugh."

"Now you see."

"After you I was in love with Evelyne Estivette's brother, Rémy, I don't know if you knew him, he was a year older than us and went to a private school in Paris. Nothing happened there either," she laughs. "In fact up until the diploma exam nothing ever happened," she says gaily.

"I see."

Marie-Thérèse sits on an arm of the chair. For a moment she does nothing, then she picks up the class photo and studies it, swinging one leg in the void. The tapping of the awning and the cries of the seagulls can be heard again. A memory flits through Adam's mind. An afternoon in the Rue Lalande, at the house of his first publisher, they were both sitting there, having exhausted all topics. In a cage some kind of exotic bird was picking out grains with its beak. Suddenly, for no reason, in a convulsive movement the bird had emitted a strident cry and then fallen silent. A mysterious call no one noticed. You look as if you've hit rock bottom, Adam.

"Is that so?"

"You look terribly depressed."

"You think so."

"Even the way you say you think so."

"Oh."

"You think so," she mimics him.

"I didn't say it like that."

"You did."

"You tell me I look depressed, I say, you think so?"

"You didn't say it like that."

"I didn't say it like that because I find it staggering that a person can come right out and tell someone they don't know at all that he looks as if he's hit rock bottom."

"I do know you."

"No, Marie-Thérèse, you don't know me at all."

"I can see clearly that you're not well. I could see that right away, back at the Jardin des Plantes."

What gives her the right to judge what state I'm in, he thinks, what gives her the right to *deliver* an assessment of the state I'm in, this limping female rat in the rain with her bags of samples. What gives her the right to decree that I'm not well, this nauseatingly robust ghost from the past. It's not that I'm not well Marie-Thérèse, I'm *extremely unwell,* I'm experiencing indescribable grief and I've no idea where consolation might come from, but you cannot know that. You cannot imagine it, Marie-Thérèse, because your energy betrays you and your courage betrays you. A being who can live in this hole without being annihilated, who can open their shutters onto this barren landscape without weeping bitter tears, cannot judge the state I'm in. A being who can face that long, narrow kitchen and that lineup of domestic appliances without feeling mortally bereft cannot judge the state I'm in. I have no admiration for your energy, it injures me. I have no admiration for your good temper, it confounds and revolts me. Nothing in you speaks to me and nothing in me can speak to you. And just because fate put me into your Jeep Wrangler today it doesn't mean you can claim the least complicity and tell me, with such gall, that I look as if I've hit rock bottom, and with what stupefying authority, that you could see clearly that I'm not well and that you'd *seen it right away* back at the Jardin des Plantes. You can understand nothing about my life because you, Marie-Thérèse, were damned from the start. You accepted this damnation and you live with it. You've blended into the mass, you've ironed out all the discords between the world and yourself, and made your nest there, you say *bottom line,* you talk about the *image* of a washing machine, you say *I have positively bloomed,* a woman who talks about *my business* with that fervor is forever alien to me. You're one of those people who never long for the impossible and one way or another have avoided expecting it. Homespun sages, I'd call you. People who *succeed* because they're *genuine* and *authentic* in a milieu in which any sensitive spirit withers and disintegrates. I refuse to believe that God has departed, leaving the field open to your sort of humanity. There's no parity between you and me. We don't resemble each other in any way, I forbid you to think we might be equals to the extent that I could allow myself to confide in you. Defeat and the sense of desolation are beyond your ken. You don't know what solitude is. You get up alone, you've no children, you've bypassed the universal model, but you do not experience *my* solitude. If you experienced it you couldn't survive for two minutes between your burrow in Viry and your operation setting up *outlets* in amusement parks. My own solitude clings to me, I'm never free of it. Whether I'm with Irène, or with the children amid the family life that'll be the death of me, in which a man only demeans himself and sells himself cheap, whether I'm in company or on my own, the feeling of solitude never leaves me. It's what rules my life. If it had ruled yours, Marie-Thérèse, you would be lying at the bottom of the lake, for you wouldn't be able to endure opening your shutters onto that dead water and those distant cries. At one moment in the Jeep you said to me: *we're not even fifty,* you said *we,* as if we were from the same stable, you

and I, as if the absurd class we were in at the lycée had
any meaning. Marie-Thérèse, I hardly remember you
at the lycée, you were the most invisible being ever.
When you came up to me with your bags of samples
and your umbrella, I pretended to be renewing a non-
existent link out of the kindness of my heart. When
in the Wrangler you said *we,* I realized my mistake,
I realized it didn't strike you as an immense honor
for me to be sitting on the seat beside you and an
immense honor that I could accept your unthinkable
invitation. Now I learn that I was not even your equal
but your protégé. I made your heart bleed, bald and
alone on my damp bench, and you loaded me into
your four-by-four the way you would one of the zoo
animals if they could be taken out of their cages. One
cannot be too wary of people of your type, suppos-
edly inoffensive people who crush one with a sen-
tence. People who bring you down in the worst
possible way, without you asking anything of them,
without you granting them the privilege of the least
familiarity, and who take advantage of your weakness
to demolish you. Marie-Thérèse, I've held on to the
naive dream of becoming a writer, that is to say a man
who tries to save himself from himself. A man who,
in order to hold on to a little momentum toward the
future, attempts to exchange his own existence for

that of words. I don't want to hear *I'm not well.* Such phrases are of abject insignificance coming from you, Marie-Thérèse. My hair is turning white, my teeth are turning yellow, and my hands are shrinking. I forbid you to notice. I'm losing my sight. I forbid you to notice. Even if I'm in the throes of death, I forbid you to notice that I'm in the throes of death, you have no right to notice anything at all about me, you can understand nothing about what I am, you have chosen to live as Marie-Thérèse Lyoc, you have chosen to be part of the hoi polloi of humanity, we do not belong to the same caste, I forbid you to notice my decline.

He gets up brusquely and says, Marie-Thérèse I must go home. She says, so soon? He replies, I can't stay any longer. She asks if he's separated from his wife. He replies that he's not separated from his wife, why should he be, and demands a taxi straightaway. Marie-Thérèse says, it's rare, you know, men who are free in the evening at the last moment. But not as rare, he feels like replying, as men capable of burying themselves alive with one great shovelful after another. Do you know a number here? he says.

"I'll take you back."

"You're not going to do the journey there and back again. Call a taxi."

"It'll cost you a fortune."

"That's not a problem."

"What's the matter with your eyes?"

"Nothing."

"You keep covering your eye with your hand."

"It's nothing."

"What is it?"

"A speck of dust, Marie-Thérèse! It'll pass."

"Don't get annoyed. Why are you shouting?"

"Call one, please."

Marie-Thérèse goes back into the room at the end of the corridor. For a moment he hears nothing. The noise of the refrigerator, birdcalls coming in waves, some of them as soft as plucked strings, voices in the fog, he thinks. He looks at the flower in its pot on the low table. He notes also, closer and barely perceptible, the crackling of the altar candle. He looks at his shoes, still damp from the rain, his trouser bottoms, too. I must go home, he thinks. Marie-Thérèse returns with a little booklet for the area. I'll try the stands, she says. I'm calling the train station, she says, dialing a number. The ringing at the other end of the line can be heard. An immediately futile ringing, he thinks, who's going to be waiting at the station terminal at night in Viry-Châtillon? Marie-Thérèse hangs up. The market terminal is hardly worth trying, she

says, dialing another number. Again a long unan-
swered ringing in the receiver. Marie-Thérèse stares
out at an opaque horizon beyond the French door on
the lake side. Then she gives up. I'll try a company in
Juvisy, she says, failing that we'll call the Taxis Bleus.
On the low table, beside the trefoil-shaped ashtray
where the black cinders have leveled off, is the tray
with the empty cherry liqueur glasses and the saucer
the Tuc crackers were on. Also the glass of water and
the torn sachet of Veinamitol. Hello, *bonsoir,* Marie-
Thérèse suddenly shouts, 2, Rue Claude-Debussy in
Viry. Viry-Châtillon, she repeats, increasing the vol-
ume by a notch. At the other end Adam can hear a
woman's voice. In Paris, shouts Marie-Thérèse. A
Xantia? She yells, fine, thanks. A gray Xantia in fifteen minutes, she says, putting down the telephone.
Another quarter of an hour, thinks Adam. She's hung
up. They're standing. Finally she says, we could sit
down for a few more minutes? She says it like a question, she doesn't dare make the decision. So they
remain standing, for even if he wanted to grant her
that little favor his knees refuse to bend and his body
to return to the armchair. A return to the armchair,
he thinks, incompatible with his wish to hurt, to indi-
cate his desire to be gone and the superior urgency of
his real life. On the other hand, he thinks, am I going

to stay on my feet for a quarter of an hour? Whether I'm sitting down or standing up the thing to be feared is time stretching out. Which, in his experience, it never does at moments of happiness. What kind of cavity in existence have I fallen into to be worrying about whether I'm sitting or standing? He sits on the very edge of the armchair, a position both uncomfortable and pathetic, he notes. He picks up the class photo, as he would pick up a brochure in a waiting room, an ultimate gesture of boredom, he thinks of the line of Borges: *the meager yesterdays of photographs.* Alice Canella is blurred. Hervé Cohen and Tristan Mateo are blurred. Demonpion, Serge Gautheron, Lyoc and Haberberg and those whose names he doesn't know, the faces studied a few moments before, are, so to speak, erased. He raises his hand. His fixation being to look with the bad eye, he raises his hand at once, but stops halfway and contents himself with shutting one eye, for Marie-Thérèse, that vulture, is observing everything, hungry for disaster, he hates her viscous solicitude, people who meddle with your health are malevolent people, people who categorize you as ill and are on the lookout for serious trouble. So he shuts one eye. And sees nothing. An indistinct gray mass. But you've never known how to wink, he tells himself, you always screwed your face up and you always saw a blur. He covers the good eye with his hand. The faces do not appear. With a beating heart he brings the photo close to the candle and receives only a vaguely turbulent impression. I'm blind, he thinks. He covers the bad eye. The faces recover their nebulous clarity. You're lucky, the optometrist had said, the vascular incident could have occurred anywhere else at all, not excluding your brain, the thrombosis could have affected a vital organ. Do we both have the same understanding of what is *vital*, Doctor? Can one even talk to people who don't consider the loss of one of one's senses as a *vital* loss? And don't you tell me you've lost only an eye, you haven't lost your sight. Someone who's lost one eye, Doctor, knows that he can lose the second, what struck the first could very well strike the second, especially in an individual suffering from a genetic anomaly, a single eye contemplating half a world is more vulnerable, besides, it's also threatened by the glaucoma, my God, the glaucoma, he thinks, what a horrible word it is too, maybe I should go tonight to get my visual field test done in the emergency room at the Quinze-Vingt eye hospital, why wait three weeks, these doctors have no sense of time. When will they understand that anxiety aggravates the disease, that waiting's a killer, waiting destroys me, Doctor, I speak as an expert, oh I've pressed my face against the glass, I did it for real at a time in my youth when I lived beside the Seine in Boulogne, I used to watch the river and the barges, I watched life passing by outside, my years were swallowed up by the void. Beside Demonpion in the photo he recognizes the hazy, puffed-up face of Nana Sitruk. What has become of Nana Sitruk, who never even got her diploma, he remembers, a housewife, a mother, a postal clerk, Nana Sitruk, vanished into life like the others, one becomes nothing, he thinks, one never becomes anything. One day, who knows, in some Jewish cemetery or other it may be possible to see the names Nana Sitruk and Adam Haberberg, engraved there in the same row, words translated from the night, monotonous stone inscriptions beneath the same sky. One day the older boy on his return from vacation had said to Irène, Mummy, you've got to tell me what you do to make people miss you so much. Nobody misses me apart from you and Daddy. He used to go to summer camp, too. He didn't like the camp but he liked the mountains. Had the boy liked the mountains? Had he liked the footpaths, the tangled roots, the thousands of pine needles? Did you like the footpaths that twist and turn who knows where, I'll wake you when I get home tonight and ask you how you run along the thorny paths. I want to see the children, I want to go home. I want to see Irène, I want to roll into a ball, curl up like a dog, its paws tucked in under its legs, I'm tired, I'm tired of falling apart, I'm afraid. Tuck me up, Irène. I don't understand what's happening to me. Marie-Thérèse has sat down on the sofa. She's lit another cigarette and says, do you want my glasses? She studies me, she observes the least of my gestures, these people who have no lives of their own dissect other people—what would I want with her glasses?

"Give me, give me the glasses!" reaching out across the table, a desperate, crustacean-like arm.

Marie-Thérèse's glasses correct the world for a moment and at once create the urge to vomit. Adam gets up. I must get some air, I'll wait outside. In the hall he puts on his coat, feels all the pockets. He already has a foot in the passageway when she says, I enjoyed seeing you again.

He descends the cold concrete staircase fast, hurtling down the steps, he passes the mailboxes, which he can read clearly, he notes, as he thrusts open the glass door. The first thing he sees outside is the white restaurant. It, too, is a little obscured by mist, but he doesn't think it's the mist in his eyes, it's the real mist of the weather. There's no longer a green sign and no longer any light behind the windows and the curtains. Almost no light around anymore, except that from the lampposts. He takes out his cell phone and calls Albert. He hears the ringing tone and then the recorded message. He says: Saint-Vaast-la-Hougue. And hangs up. He walks at random toward the parking lot. He hears the sounds of several cars in the distance. None of them approaches. He walks at random toward the lake. Where are the birds, he thinks, still making his way toward the dark expanse. He crosses the Sunday strollers' pathway, that's the name he gives it, and almost falls, as he steps over the useless parapet. He follows the grassy slope that plunges down into the water. A scent of undergrowth hangs in the air, is it the night or the fog, a scent of damp earth and water lilies. He thinks of water lilies lining fast-flowing rivers, of trees laid flat, who knows why, torn up by the wind or struck by lightning. He thinks of water lilies growing amid dead boughs, countless branches, dead and peeling. He remembers the solitary animal from the forests of Asia. One day I'll go into the mountain forests of Asia, he thinks. And then he sees them. Tucked in close to one bank, huddled together, sleeping perhaps, ducks, swans, and possibly other kinds of birds, it's a closed book to him. Adam walks closer. And then, is it because of his eyes, the darkness, or the mist, all he can see now is a petrified, downy mass.

When the car arrives at the parking lot Adam doesn't hear it. What he hears is his name. His name tossed onto the breeze, brazenly proclaimed on all sides, and he feels the same pang as years ago at Suresnes when his mother shouted Adam out of the window. This shout simultaneously revealed his name, his window, the time for his bath or his homework, and his mother's voice and face, and he was the only one to be summoned like that right in the middle of a game, right in the middle of a chase, and if he was not the only one he was always the first one to be summoned, he remembers, and the only one in that extra-shrill voice that mortified him. Marie-Thérèse is on her balcony half hidden by the cement balustrade. She's pointing to the taxi down below. When will she stop being there? He slips on the slope, crosses the Sunday strollers' pathway, and heads straight for the Xantia. He says, Rue Morère, in the fourteenth, by the Porte de Châtillon. The woman starts the car and goes into a sweeping U-turn in the parking lot. Adam looks at the meter, the back of the woman's neck, the puppet dangling from the rearview mirror. He sees the Jeep Wrangler, the darkness over the lake as they go by. He lifts his head. On the empty terrace that looks immense Marie-Thérèse Lyoc is waving good-bye. A signal he would have been unaware of, he thinks, had he not looked up, and which would then have been addressed to nobody. He lowers the window to put his arm out, she can't see him inside the car, he thinks, but the vehicle accelerates and his own gesture traces a line in the void.

Adam lays his head back on the seat, his eyes closed. The green shoe has disappeared. In its place he thinks he can see alternating black and white squares at the end of a dark road. Over the course of several years, he reflects, sitting there in the Xantia as it climbs the slope and turns off who knows where, he used to play chess with Goncharki, each of them believing himself superior to the other. As their sessions continued Goncharki had gotten into the habit of sprinkling himself before every game with Penhaligon's Blenheim Bouquet, Churchill's perfume. One day, unable to stand it any longer, Adam had said, I'm suffocating, I can't go on playing in these conditions. A warrior's perfume, Goncharki had calmly replied, moving his castle. A cheat's perfume, Adam had retorted. A cheat? Yes. You drench yourself on purpose to distract me. Pathetic, Goncharki had concluded, laying down his king. He would have to talk to Guen about this succession of visions. Should any significance be

attributed to them beyond the physiological? A shoe
and a chessboard. Don't tell me, Professor (now I've
lost my left eye you're the only person I want to deal
with), that the body fashions images at random, don't
tell me, because you know nothing about it, that it's
purely a matter of chance, when we close our eyes,
whether we see a shoe or a chessboard. On the day
of Winston Churchill's funeral Goncharki's father,
hunched beside his radio set, following the whole
ceremony over the air and frowning at the smallest
noise, had looked up and said: "God is not as great as
Churchill." It was not so much the extravagance of
the remark that had struck Goncharki at the age of
thirteen as the expression of ferocious perspicacity
and also, he felt he could perceive, of condemnation
that accompanied it. It was, he had related, a *verdict*
in the cosmic sense. Goncharki's book on Meyer Lansky began with these words: "Night falls in the sad
Florida apartment that has no view and only one bedroom with twin beds." Adam liked this lame sen-
tence, which came to him who knows why. What
story could you tell, he thinks, you have no story to
tell, and what's more you've never been able to tell
stories, let alone make them up, even for your children, people say you're a writer and you don't even
know how to tell your children a story, no you don't,

you don't know how to come up with events, obstacles, sudden reversals, you surprised yourself with *The Black Prince of Mea-Hor* but Blade is immortal, you don't tell an immortal's life story, the truth about immortals is that they have no life story. You make up adventures, nothing more, anyone can do that.

ALSO BY YASMINA REZA

"Cantankerous, funny and fierce. . . . A stark yet bleakly comic look at the limitations and solitude inherent in the human condition." —Los Angeles Times

DESOLATION

Samuel Perlman, the elderly narrator of Yasmina Reza's deliriously dyspeptic novel, is surrounded by happy people. His wife, Nancy, is thrilled to be a member of the human race. His grown son is content crisscrossing the world to "sample exotic fruit with the savages." But Samuel himself refuses to be happy and his attempt to explain his refusal (half to his son and half to himself) generates an epic, blasphemous, and hilarious rant against the compromises of his life. Whether he is recounting his pal Lionel's heroic battle against impotence; lamenting the loss of his great love, the irresistible Marisa Botton; or pondering the possibility of a new love in the person of one Genevieve Abramowitz, the droll, irascible Perlman is one of the great talkers of contemporary fiction. And *Desolation* is one of the most dazzling performances ever written for one voice.

Fiction/Literature/978-0-375-72472-5

VINTAGE BOOKS
Available at your local bookstore, or visit
www.randomhouse.com